D0463959

Willow King

Race the Wind

Willow King

Race the Wind

Chris Platt

Random House Riders

Random House 🏠 New York

Jacket art by Joanie Schwarz
Jacket design by Georgia Morrissey
Interior design by Gretchen Schuler

Copyright © 2000 by Chris Platt
Jacket art copyright © 2000 by Joanie Schwarz
All rights reserved under International and Pan-American Copyright Conventions.
Published in the United States by Random House, Inc., New York,
and simultaneously in Canada by Random House of Canada Limited, Toronto.

www.randomhouse.com/kids

Library of Congress Cataloging-in-Publication Data
Platt, Chris, 1959-
Willow King: race the wind/by Chris Platt
p. cm — (Random House riders)
Summary: Determined to ride her horse in the Kentucky Derby despite her physical
handicap, Katie overcomes great obstacles and even helps a blind girl face her own
kind of challenge.
ISBN 0-679-88657-5 (trade) — ISBN 0-679-98657-X (lib. bdg.)
[1. Determination (Personality trait)–Fiction. 2. Horses–Fiction. 3. Horse racing–
Fiction. 4. Physically handicapped–Fiction.] 1. Title.
PZ7.P7123115 W1 2000
[Fic]–dc21
99-56117

Printed in the United States of America
March 2000
10 9 8 7 6 5 4 3 2 1
RANDOM HOUSE and colophon are registered trademarks
of Random House, Inc.

Dedicated to
my grandmother
Jane Kelley
and my mother
Sue Smith.

All that is good in me
has come from you.

Willow King

Race the Wind

✦ Chapter One ✦

"Hold him, Katie!" Jason Roberts yelled as he maneuvered his paint gelding next to the two-year-old Thoroughbred colt Katie Durham was riding. "Don't let him buck. Keep his head up!"

Katie braced herself as Willow's Destiny rose high into the air and came down in a straight-legged, bone-jarring bump. Katie's teeth clacked together from the impact.

Willow's Destiny was a full brother to Katie's champion racehorse, Willow King. But at the moment, Katie couldn't see anything the two horses had in common.

She gasped as the chestnut-colored colt dove to the side to avoid the pickup horse. "I'm trying to get his head up. You think I'm enjoying this?" Katie grouched as the colt increased his speed and bucked harder.

Her arms ached from trying to raise the rampaging colt's head. She didn't know how much longer she could hold out. Destiny wanted her off his back. She thought about jumping, but one look at the dirt track as it passed under the horse's hooves made her reconsider. Jumping usually resulted in broken bones. She looked to Jason for help, but she knew that Destiny's head was too low for Jason to move in with the pickup horse and grab a rein. Her only hope was to keep her balance until the colt wore himself out.

Destiny bucked again, and the sharp snap of splitting leather filled the air. Katie had only seconds to untangle her hands from the reins before the saddle's girth gave way. She was thrown over the horse's head with the next buck.

As she somersaulted over Destiny's head, Katie watched images pass her like a slow-motion movie. She saw the look of anguish on Jason's face as he reined in his horse to keep from trampling her. She saw old John, the trainer, and Tom Ellis, the stable owner, vaulting over the fence to come to her rescue. Over it all, she saw the smug face of Cindy Ellis, smirking by the racetrack's rail.

Katie hit the ground hard and rolled in the damp sand. After tumbling to a stop, she lay faceup in the middle of the track, gasping for air. She was fifteen years old and had never broken a bone. She prayed this wouldn't be the first time.

Opening her eyes, Katie waited for her vision to clear. The puffy gray clouds of the Oregon sky gradually came into focus. She lay still, waiting for the hurt to descend on her like a herd of wild horses. Surprisingly, she couldn't feel anything, which scared her more than the prospect of pain. Being paralyzed as the result of a riding accident was a frightening thought.

"Katie, are you all right?"

Jason's red-gold hair swam into her vision. She squinted, then drew a quick gulp of air, choking on the gritty sand that lodged in her teeth and throat. A sharp stab of pain raced down her back. It settled into a dull ache, which seemed to envelop her entire body. Katie sighed with relief. Pain meant her spine wasn't broken.

Katie blinked hard, and Jason's face suddenly came into focus, appearing upside down. The angle made his grimace look like a grin, and Katie laughed.

"Are you crazy? How can you laugh at a time like this? You could have been killed!" Jason snapped.

Katie just laughed again. A year ago, she'd had a childish crush on Jason. He was a year older than she, and Katie had liked his nice smile, his easygoing manner, and his way with horses. He had become a great ally, helping her break her Thoroughbred, Willow King. It was with Jason's aid that she'd been able to see King win the Portland Downs Futurity. Now they were close, and their friendship was blossoming into something bigger and better as they worked toward getting Willow King ready for the Kentucky Derby.

Except for this minor wreck, life was great.

Old John reached them and knelt in the sand at Katie's head. He brushed the hair from her brow and checked for broken bones.

"Is she going to be okay?" Jason hovered over Katie's prone form.

"Calm down, lad," Mr. Ellis said as he helped the trainer examine Katie. "You're a mighty lucky girl. Everything seems to be intact." He pulled her gently to her feet.

"I don't feel too lucky." Katie hobbled around, making sure everything still worked. She pulled off her right boot, turning it upside down to dislodge the stones it had gathered in her fall. The orthopedic lift she wore in her shoe because of her short leg tumbled out with the stones. Katie snatched the red rubber piece from the ground and shoved it back in her boot. Everyone here knew she had one leg shorter than the other, but Katie still felt uncomfortable about it.

John dusted the wet sand from her back. "This girl thinks she's too hardheaded to get hurt," John scolded. "I know you're tough, missy, but I want you to take the next couple of days off." At Katie's frown, John continued, "And don't let me catch you sneaking in here trying to clean stalls or move hay. You're to take the next few days off, and that's an order."

"Yes, sir." Katie rubbed her legs and stretched her back. At the moment, that sounded like a pretty good idea.

The outrider returned with the wayward colt. John gathered the reins, and Mr. Ellis picked up the broken saddle. Together they headed back to the barn. When they were out of earshot, Jason turned to Katie.

"Geez, Kat, you sure know how to scare a guy." He removed his black hat and slapped it against his leg.

"How touching," Cindy Ellis scoffed as she popped her riding crop against her shiny black boots. She impatiently flipped her long blond braid over her shoulder and dusted imaginary lint from her new riding breeches.

Katie groaned. She had forgotten that Cindy was standing by the rail.

"That was quite a show, Katie. Maybe now my dad will see what a mistake it was to let you get a gallop license."

Jason frowned. "At least Katie *has* a gallop license."

Cindy gripped the handle of her whip and turned a

pretty shade of pink. "Nobody asked you, Jason. You can climb right back on your horse and leave."

"Have you forgotten that I'm John's assistant trainer now?" Jason returned. "I've got a right to be here."

Katie stepped between the two. "Come on, guys, we're all working toward the same goal. We all want to see Willow King make it to the Kentucky Derby."

"I'm not so sure of that." Jason eyed Cindy suspiciously, then moved to where his paint gelding was tied to the fence.

Katie frowned. Jason was probably right. She thought about all the times the owner's daughter had jealously tried to sabotage Willow King's chances of winning. But that was in the past. They had to put it behind them and go forward. "Let's just forget everything and call it a day, okay? I'm tired and I want to go home." Katie limped off the track.

"You're right," Cindy said with a smile. "There's no need for all of us to fight. Take a couple of extra days off if you need to."

Katie was immediately suspicious of Cindy's kind words. Old John liked to say, "Never look a gift horse in the mouth," but when Cindy Ellis was uncharacteristically generous, something was up. However, Katie didn't have the will or the energy to figure it out. "I think I might do that," Katie said as she unsnapped the chin strap of her hard hat, pulled the helmet from her head, and shook her long brown curls over her shoulders. "As quick as I'm stiffening up, I'll probably need a few extra days to recover."

"Cindy!" Mr. Ellis yelled from the top barn. "Get up to the house and help your mother prepare for our visitor."

"Visitor?" Katie asked.

Cindy made a face. "Yeah. We've got someone coming

to stay with us for a while. You two should have a lot in common. I'll bring her down to the barn when she gets here."

"Great, I'll look forward to meeting her."

"Don't count on it." Cindy smirked, then walked off, leaving Katie to stare after her.

"What was that all about?" Jason asked as he came to stand beside her.

"Did you know the Ellises are going to have a long-term visitor?"

"No, this is the first I've heard of it."

"It's a girl. I don't know how old she is, but Cindy said we'd have a lot in common, so she must be close to our age."

Jason watched the farm owner's daughter disappear around the barn. "Let's hope she doesn't take after Cindy. She could be trouble."

"Trouble?" Katie laughed. "What could be worse than Cindy?"

Jason paused as if deep in thought. Then a small grin tugged at the corner of his mouth. "I think I see your point." He joined her laughter. "Come on, Kat," he said as he clapped her on the back, then smiled apologetically when she winced. "Let me give you a ride home. You don't look like you're up to the walk."

"Thanks, I'll take you up on that, but I want to stop by Willow King's stall first. I'll meet you at your truck in five minutes." She waved to Jason and turned up the aisle where her horse was stabled.

Katie smiled as Willow King poked his beautiful bay head over the stall door and nickered a greeting. He pressed his muzzle against her jacket pockets, searching for a treat.

"Sorry, ol' boy," Katie said as she rubbed the white star in the center of the three-year-old colt's forehead and parted his black forelock. "No treats today. I'm heading home. Your little brother was a real terror today. He bucked me off, and now everyone is worried about me, so I have to go home."

Katie readjusted her stance to take some of the pressure off her bad leg. "You know what it's like, don't you, boy," She said as she stepped gingerly toward the hay pile and grabbed a handful of alfalfa to feed him.

She smiled proudly as she studied the handsome brown colt. Willow King had been foaled right at Tom Ellis's Willow Run Farm. But the bay colt had been born with crooked legs, and Mr. Ellis wanted him destroyed. Katie had felt an immediate kinship with the colt and asked Mr. Ellis to sell her the new foal. After much begging and pleading, the farm owner agreed, and Willow King and his mother came to live at the Durhams' small farm just down the road.

Katie removed Willow King's leather halter with the brass nameplate and hung it on a hook outside his stall. She leaned her head against the barn wall and breathed a contented sigh as King nuzzled her cheek and blew soft breaths into her hair. It had been a long three years, filled with heartaches and hard lessons, but King had grown into a magnificent horse and was now on the path to the Kentucky Derby!

A horn blared, warning Katie that Jason was ready to leave. "I've got to go," she whispered to King as she snatched another handful of alfalfa and offered it to his outstretched lips. "I've got to rest up so I can get back to galloping you in a few days. I need to get in lots of practice." She took King's muzzle in her hands and placed a kiss on the tip of his nose, laughing when the horse raised his lip to show she had tickled him. "Someday, when I'm good enough, I'm going to be your jockey."

Jason honked again, and Katie gave the colt a good-bye pat, then hustled down the shed row as fast as she could.

"Another rider?" Katie hollered into the phone as she sat up in bed and flopped back against the headboard. "I've only been gone three days, and they've *replaced* me already?"

"Somebody had to gallop him," said Jan's reasoning voice over the phone line. "You didn't think they'd give Willow King a vacation just because you got hurt, did you? He's in training for the Kentucky Derby. Be sensible, Katie. You'll be riding him as soon as you get back. Besides, this guy is really nice…and he's cute."

Katie scowled. Somebody new was riding King, and all her best friend could say was "he's cute." "Okay, I know you're dying to tell me all about it. What's up?"

"His name is Mark, and he's seventeen," Jan said. "He's a senior at our school, and his family just moved here from the East Coast. He was a jockey back in New York, and he just started riding at Portland Downs."

Katie groaned. Maybe he was trying to take over her job.

"Since he's going to the same school we are, I'm sure we'll see a lot of him," continued Jan. "I hope you like him."

"Just as long as he doesn't get too attached to King," Katie said.

"Katie, you *do* need a jockey for Willow King. Your regular jockey still hasn't healed from the spill he took last month. I hear his leg is in a cast, and he's still on crutches. He's going to be out for a while. Just give Mark a chance. He really is a good rider."

Katie was silent for a moment. She hadn't mentioned it to anyone, but she was considering getting her jockey's license. And why not? She had been galloping horses in the morning for almost a year now. She'd be sixteen in another month—old enough to try for her apprentice jockey's license. She knew several retired jockeys who would help her learn the ropes. Maybe even the new kid would be able to help her.

"Hello? Earth to Katie," Jan's voice boomed over the line.

"Sorry, I was just thinking. Listen, I've got an appointment with my physical therapist later today. If he says it's okay to ride, I'll be there tomorrow."

"Is your back really bad?" Jan asked in sympathy.

"You know how it gets when my hips are knocked out of alignment," Katie said. "It hurts a lot."

"Let's hope the doc can get you put back together right," Jan said encouragingly. "Everyone misses you."

"Even Cindy?" Katie laughed.

"Well, maybe not everyone." Jan joined in the humor. "She's been trying to talk her father into letting her gallop King while you're out."

Katie almost choked. "You're joking, right?"

"No, I'm not. Fortunately, Mark came along about the time she was wearing her father down, so he got to ride King instead."

"I owe him for that." Katie switched the phone to her other ear. It had been bad enough when Cindy was riding Katie's show horse, Jester. Katie didn't want to think about the damage Cindy could do to King. The thought sent shivers down her spine. She knew she had to get out of bed–King's career depended on it. "I'll see you tomorrow, Jan."

Katie hung up the phone and carefully lowered her feet to the floor. Her spine cracked and popped. She hoped Dr. Marty could work a miracle today. That was the only way she'd be riding by tomorrow.

She shrugged gingerly into her jeans and sweatshirt. After donning her socks, Katie picked up her orthopedic shoe and paused for a moment. She hated that thing and what it represented. Why couldn't she be *normal* like everyone else? If it weren't for her legs, she would have been back to work already.

Katie heaved the hated shoe across the room. It crashed against the door and dropped to the carpet. A moment later, the door opened and her mother peeked around the corner. Katie could see the puzzled look on her face.

Peg Durham picked up the shoe, then crossed the room and sat on the bed next to Katie. "You haven't been this out of sorts in a long time. What's up?"

"Somebody else is riding Willow King," Katie said flatly. She could feel the hurt and anger building inside. She bit her lip to keep from screaming.

"I understand how that might upset you, but other people have ridden King before. What's different about this time?" Mrs. Durham turned the shoe over in her hands.

Katie shrugged her shoulders and looked away. Her mother wouldn't understand.

"Come on, honey, I know when something is really eating at you. It won't do any good to keep it locked up." She tucked one of Katie's unruly brown curls behind her ear. "Katie, you know you've always been able to talk to me."

Katie took the shoe from her mother, frowning as she turned it over in her hands. "I'm tired of my stupid leg, Mom. Okay?"

There, she'd said it. Katie knew she wouldn't see surprise or shock on her mother's face. They'd been down this road before.

Mrs. Durham stroked her daughter's hair. "I know it's hard for you at times, but, Katie, you've come so far and accomplished so much. There are other kids who have a lot more difficult things to deal with."

Katie remembered the moment of fear she had experienced when she lay in the middle of the racetrack and couldn't feel her limbs. She thought of the jockeys she had seen in wheelchairs. "You're right. I'm just feeling bad because there's a new kid at the barn, and he's riding Willow King. And he's a real jockey."

"But you *need* a jockey for King. Maybe this boy will be the right one," Mrs. Durham said.

Katie bent to put on her shoes, debating whether she should tell her mother about her secret dream of becoming a jockey. She straightened and looked her mother square in the eye. "I was kinda hoping that *I* could be King's jockey this year." She bit her bottom lip, knowing that her mother was going to disapprove of such a dangerous occupation.

Mrs. Durham tucked a curl behind Katie's ear and smiled softly. "I wondered when you would bring up this subject," she said. "I didn't think you'd be content to be just an exercise rider for much longer."

Katie felt her mouth drop open and quickly snapped it shut. "You mean you've known that I wanted to be a jockey, and you don't mind?"

Mrs. Durham rose from the bed and straightened the horse figurines on Katie's bookshelf. "I can't say that I'm not concerned. Those are awfully big animals, and they're traveling very fast. You've seen some of the accidents, Katie. But being a jockey is the next step up from galloping in the mornings, and knowing you like I do…" She smiled her motherly smile. "It's the logical next step."

Katie grinned her thanks, but the brightness dimmed as a dark thought crossed her mind.

"What's the matter, dear? You're going to be riding in the Kentucky Derby. You should be jumping up and down."

Katie jammed her hands deep into the pockets of her jeans and scuffed her foot across an irregular seam in the carpet. This was hard to admit, but she had to express her fears to somebody. She had really wanted to talk to Jan about it this morning, but her friend had been too wrapped up in the new boy to talk seriously.

"Come on, spit it out," Mrs. Durham ordered.

Katie lowered her head and mumbled.

"Speak up, honey, I can't understand a word you're saying."

Katie met her mother's level gaze. "What if I can't do it, Mom? What if I can't pass the jockey test? There are only seven more weeks until the Derby."

Peg Durham crossed the few feet between them and placed her hands on Katie's shoulders. "You remember what your father used to say. 'Sweetie, you can do anything you want. All you've got to do is put your mind to it.'"

Katie thought of her father, who had passed away when she was eight. She wished he were still there. At times like this, she missed him more than ever.

"Look at how far you've come," her mother continued. "Remember, success isn't just measured in whether you win or lose. I'm so proud of everything you've accomplished. Whether you get your jockey's license or not, I'll be just as proud of you as I always am."

Katie hugged her mother. "You're the best, Mom."

Katie forced a smile, but in her heart the doubt loomed as big as ever.

Could she get her jockey's license in time for the Kentucky Derby?

⇌ *Chapter Two* ⇌

"Katie, you're here!" Jan gave her a hug and walked her down the shed row. "The way you talked yesterday, I thought it would be at least a week before we'd see you back at the barn."

Katie stopped in front of Willow King's stall. "I told you Dr. Marty was a miracle worker."

At the sound of her voice, King's head popped up from the straw he had been sorting through in an effort to find a stem of hay. He nickered his greeting and poked his head over the stall door.

"You know you ate it all last night, and you're not getting any more until after the morning workout." Katie chuckled as she traced her fingers over the swirl of white hairs in the small star on King's forehead. "But if you promise not to tell, I've got a little something for those hunger pangs."

Katie reached into her pocket and withdrew a small carrot. While King munched happily, she buried her face in his sleek brown coat, breathing in his warm horse scent. She had been away from King only for a few days, but it had almost seemed like an eternity.

Katie closed her eyes and listened to the sound of the training barn. Stall doors clanged as horses were led to the cross-ties to be saddled for their morning workouts; the purr of the hotwalker engine sifted over the singing of a groom who was cleaning stalls; the quick staccato stride of an exercise rider echoed down the barn as he hurried to catch his next mount; the pounding of hooves grew louder as a horse moved down the back side of the racetrack, then faded into nothingness as the animal rounded the turn.

Katie *loved* this place. What would she do if she couldn't ride? She hoped she never had to find out.

Jan broke into her reverie. "Katie, Mark is here this morning. Jason told John he didn't think you'd be back for a few more days, so John asked Mark to come by this morning for Willow King."

Katie tried to hide her disappointment, but she knew Jan would see right through it. They had been best friends for too long for Jan not to know how much she wanted to ride King. Katie put on a smile. After all, it was only for today. She would be back in the irons tomorrow.

"So where is this boy wonder?" Katie asked.

Jan looked at her watch. "John told him to be here by eight o'clock."

As if on cue, the boy in question rounded the corner of the barn. He strode confidently toward them, his riding crop popping smartly against his knee-high gallop boots. He stopped in front of Katie and extended his hand.

"Hi, I'm Mark. You must be Katie."

The jockey's smile was so dazzling, Katie almost forgot to shake his hand. She had been prepared not to like the kid, but he was nothing like what she had pictured. To start with, he was at least five inches taller than she was. When Katie thought of a jockey, she always expected to see a short guy who was skinny enough to disappear when he turned sideways. Mark was slender, but that seemed to be his natural build rather than the result of days or weeks of starving himself to make race weight.

Most of the jockeys for Willow Run Farm bore premature lines on their faces from the rigors of the job and the constant exposure to the hot summer sun and cold winter wind. Mark's face was unlined except for the small dimple in his right cheek. A lock of blond hair escaped from under his riding helmet and feathered over his startlingly blue eyes. And his smile was nothing less than mesmerizing.

Katie heard the tail end of a question and suddenly realized that she had been staring so hard, she hadn't even noticed Mark was speaking to her.

She quickly dropped his hand and backed up a step, her eyes cutting to Jan. She ignored her friend's smirk. "I...I'm sorry, could you repeat that, please?" Katie could feel the hot blush of embarrassment flood her cheeks. She turned and busied herself with King's tack while she awaited the question.

"I said, since you're feeling better, does that mean you're going to ride King today?" He grabbed the saddle from her hands and placed it on the rack.

Katie refused to look in his eyes. She didn't want him to see how desperately she wanted to ride her horse. She knew that he had made a special trip to gallop King, and it was only fair that he get to do it. She was also afraid that if she looked at him again, she'd be caught up in that brilliant smile, and she'd make a fool of herself once more. Jan had said the boy was cute, but Katie hadn't expected him to be *this* cute.

"No, no," Katie stammered. "John said you were going to ride today. I'll get King ready to go." She accidentally dropped the saddle cloth and quickly bent to pick it up. What was the matter with her? Why was her heart galloping in her chest? This was just a guy.

He's very cute, and he's a successful jockey, but you're acting like someone hit you over the head with an idiot stick, she chided herself.

"Katie, it's great to have you back!" Jason's long-legged stride carried him quickly down the aisle. "I didn't expect you for a few more days. We asked Mark to gallop King today."

Katie peeked around Jason's tall form and encountered Mark's smiling blue eyes. She averted her gaze and turned to enter King's stall, but not before seeing the questioning look Jason gave her.

"I guess you two have already been introduced?" Jason asked as he ran a hand through his short red-gold hair.

Jan stepped forward, handing Katie a halter and lead rope. "Been there, done that," she said.

"Good. Then let's all get down to business." Jason entered King's stall and handed Katie the saddle, giving her a smile as he did so. "It's good to have you back, Kat."

Katie breathed a little easier. Jason was like a compass. He always steered her in the right direction when she was out of whack. She returned his smile. Once she immersed herself in her work, she could forget about Mark and the fool she had made of herself.

"Are you okay with this, Katie?" Jason asked as he helped her place the pads on King's back. "You seem kind of out of sorts. If you want, I'll put Mark up on another horse and you can ride King."

Katie smiled. "Thanks, but Mark's here and he's ready to go. Everyone's been bragging about him. I'd like to see how he does."

"Well, we do need to find another jockey. And he might be the one." Jason rested his arm on King's hindquarters and watched Katie check her tack.

"So I hear." Katie frowned and pulled the girth up tight. King swished his tail, showing his disapproval. He was used to having the girth snugged a little at a time. "Sorry, fella."

Jason was giving Katie that funny look again. Did she dare tell him about her plan to get a jockey's license? She didn't like to keep secrets from him, but something told her to keep this under her helmet a while longer. If she failed, the fewer people who knew, the better.

Jason opened the stall door. "You lead him out, and I'll give Mark a leg up."

Mark smiled at Katie as she stepped out of the stall. She returned the smile, then quickly looked away, intent on adjusting King's bridle.

Jason boosted the boy into the saddle. "If you can handle it from here, I'll get Digger ready for his workout."

Katie led them to the track, guiding King by the chin strap, while Mark adjusted his irons and knotted the reins.

"Were you the last one to ride in this saddle?" Mark asked.

"Yeah. None of the other riders like it because it's old. But I think it's broken in just right."

"I see you like to ride acey-deucey," he said, referring to the way some riders hike their outside stirrup an inch or two higher than the inside one so that they can lean into the turns with their mounts.

Katie paused a moment. "Well…I don't really ride that way. It's just that…that…my right leg is a little shorter than my left, so when I pull my outside iron up, it balances me out."

"Oh. You've got a built-in acey-deucey. That's cool."

She didn't think it was very cool, but it was nice of him to say so.

Katie concentrated hard on putting one foot in front of the other, trying to smooth out her usual awkward gait. She didn't know why she cared what this new guy thought, but memories of students at school calling her "gimp-along Katie" sat heavily on her mind.

"Hello, *hello*. Mark to Katie. Are you there?"

Katie realized that Mark had asked her another question that she hadn't heard. *He must think I'm a real lamebrain,* she thought.

"Sorry," Katie apologized. "I was off in space again."

"I do that myself, but I've realized it's not too smart to do that around these animals."

"You're right about that," Katie said. "When King was a yearling, I was swimming him at the horse pool down the road. I was daydreaming about something…" She decided not to mention that the daydream was about Jason. "King swam too close and got wrapped around the podium stand. He almost drowned before I got him undone."

"Wow," Mark said as he reached down and patted King's sleek neck. "To think you almost lost a potential

19

Derby winner."

Katie looked up in surprise. "How did you know we were pointing him toward the Derby?"

"Shoot, girl, it doesn't take long for word like that to travel, and I always aim for the best horse in the stable." Mark stood in the irons, measuring to see if they were the right length. "It's always been my dream to win the Kentucky Derby."

Katie studied him for a moment. Mark was confident and determined. Suddenly Katie wondered if she was up to butting heads with this boy. King could only have *one* jockey.

When they arrived at the track entrance, Mark smooched the colt into a trot and looked back over his shoulder. "How do you want him to go today?"

"Just an easy gallop once around," Katie said. "Trot him back almost to the finish line. That'll give him about a mile-and-a-half workout."

Katie watched them trot off, then walked to her favorite spot on the rail. It wasn't raining this morning, though the sky threatened to spill at any time. She waved to a couple of the grooms who were watching the workouts from the warmth of the spectators' box which stood ten feet above the railing just outside the exit gate.

Katie directed her attention back to Willow King. Mark had just reached the finish line and was turning the colt when Cindy's voice interrupted her concentration.

"I see Mark is riding your horse today. Is this a permanent switch?"

She said it innocently enough, but Katie could hear the underlying barb. Why couldn't Cindy just leave her alone?

Was she still mad because her father had cut his lease short on Katie's show horse, Jester, and given him back to Katie? Cindy had treated Jester badly, so it was no surprise she hadn't done well on him in the shows, despite the fact that Katie had won ribbons on him all the time over the last few years. Why couldn't Cindy just let it go?

"I think Mark is an excellent rider," Cindy continued. "My dad says he would be a good replacement jockey for King. We're going to put Mark on our own stock. Willow King is entered Wednesday night, which would be a good time to try Mark out." Cindy waited anxiously for Katie's reply.

"This is the first time I've seen him ride," Katie said as she watched King gallop down the back side of the track. He tossed his head and cantered sideways, trying to un-balance his rider so he could take the bit and run. For a moment, she thought it might work, but Mark pulled the slack from the reins and bowed King's neck. The colt responded by lining out and establishing a nice rhythmic gait.

"He knows his stuff," Katie said. "But I'm not sure yet who'll be riding King in the races." That wasn't a lie. Katie really didn't know who would ride her horse. She just omit-ted the fact that it might be her. For now, ol' blabbermouth Cindy didn't need to know about her plan to get a jockey's license. It was going to be tough enough as it was. She didn't need extra obstacles thrown in her path by a jealous rival.

As Mark galloped by, he looked over at the girls and smiled.

"Daddy says he's going to be one of the hottest jockeys

at Portland Downs this spring," Cindy said, flipping her blond braid over her shoulder and brushing the bangs from her eyes. "You'd be a fool not to use him, Katie."

"We'll see. I want to make sure Mark gets along well with King." Katie knew it would take some time before she could get her license. Until then, it wouldn't hurt to consider Mark as Willow King's temporary jockey. The rider they had been planning to use wasn't anything special. Maybe she would think about giving Mark a chance.

Katie watched King go by for the second time. With his workout complete, Mark looked back over his shoulder to make sure there were no horses nearby, then eased the colt to the outside rail, where they stopped and stood facing the inner rail. Mark patted him on the neck and turned to leave the track.

Katie caught King's chin strap as they stepped through the track exit. "What do you think?" she asked.

Mark smiled down at her as he patted King again. "This is one fine piece of hide. I'd sure like to be the one to ride him in his next race. I know I could get him to the winner's circle for you."

"I told Katie she'd be crazy not to use you," Cindy said, scrambling to catch up with them. "Willow King will be the first horse that Willow Run Farm has entered in the Kentucky Derby. You know my father bred this horse, don't you?"

Mark looked at Cindy, then at Katie. "I didn't know that. I thought Katie raised him."

"I did, but he's off this farm," Katie confirmed. "That's why I called him *Willow* King."

Mark appeared to be baffled by her answer. "But Tom

Ellis seems to be a pretty good judge of horseflesh. I can't believe he'd let this colt slip away from him," Mark said as he unknotted the reins.

Cindy bristled. "Daddy's an excellent judge of horses. He just wasn't thinking when he practically gave this horse to Katie. I think he felt sorry for her and her mother because they were ready to lose their ranch. He's too bighearted for his own good." She pouted prettily as she stared up at Mark.

Katie grimaced. Leave it to Cindy to bring up a sore subject and distort the truth. "To be fair to Mr. Ellis, he's a very good judge of horses. It's just that King wasn't exactly a prime specimen when he was born."

Mark smiled encouragingly. "How's that?"

When the young jockey smiled at her like that, Katie's heart did a little flip-flop. She opened her mouth to reply, but Cindy cut her off.

"King was born with the crookedest legs you ever saw. Nobody thought he'd be able to stand and nurse. It was better to put him down than have him starve to death." Cindy shot Katie a scathing glance. "Katie didn't bother to tell my father that King had already stood and nursed, so when she begged him for the colt, Dad gave him up without a fight."

"That's not exactly how it went," Katie said, amazed at the lengths Cindy would go to put her down. "I told Mr. Ellis that the colt had nursed, but he said that even if King did pull through, his legs would never straighten enough for him to amount to anything. John, our trainer, had faith in the colt and helped me save him. Mr. Ellis agreed to trade him for a lease on my show horse, Jester."

Mark pulled King to a stop and vaulted from the saddle. He knelt in front of the horse and ran a hand down his front legs, then whistled and looked up at Katie. "You'd never know that these legs were anything but straight. How'd you do it?"

Katie wanted out of this conversation before Cindy could make any more false accusations. "It's a trade secret," she said with a grin.

Mark laughed. "So that's how it's going to be?" He loosened King's girth and slapped him on the haunches. "I guess the rest of this story will have to wait until another day. I've got another mount to catch." He tipped his hard hat. "Ladies."

"Wait!" Cindy trailed after him. "I want to talk about some riding lessons. I'm trying to get my gallop license, and there's nobody good enough around here to learn from." She looked pointedly at Katie. "Why don't you come up to the house when you're done, Mark, and we'll talk about it?"

"Sure." Mark nodded his good-bye, then turned and ran down the shed row to catch his next mount.

Cindy curled her lips in a mock smile. "It won't be long until I'll be riding on the big track with you."

Katie bit back a comment about buying extra life insurance. She had learned that it didn't do any good to taunt Cindy Ellis. "I'm sure Mark will be an excellent teacher," she replied in an even tone.

Mark would probably be more than happy to teach a pretty little rich girl how to ride, Katie thought. Especially since her father owned some of the best horses in the state. He'd be crazy to turn it down. Still, the thought bothered her. Cindy always got what she wanted.

"Well, I'm going to run up to the house and round up our new guest," Cindy said. "She needs some fresh air. You won't mind keeping her company while I talk to Mark, will you, Katie? Camela can be a real pain sometimes."

"Sure, bring her on down," Katie offered.

"Thanks, Katie. You're a real pal."

Katie turned King toward the barn. She wished Cindy had meant that last remark. But Katie knew from experience that she was only considered a "pal" when Cindy wanted a favor.

Twenty minutes later, Katie had just finished raking the shed row when a tapping noise caught her attention. She paused, listening to the constant *tock, tock, tap* as it drifted closer. Several of the horses heard the foreign noise and left their feed buckets to peer over the tops of their stall doors.

In another moment, Cindy appeared around the corner. She was holding the arm of a pretty, petite blond girl who appeared to be a couple of years younger than the two of them. Katie guessed that she was about thirteen. The tapping sound came from the white cane that the girl clung to, swinging it from side to side as she advanced down the aisle. They stopped ten feet from Katie.

"Well, here she is," Cindy announced with a sweep of her arm. "Katie, this is Camela. Camela, this is Katie."

"Pamela?"

"No, Camela," Cindy corrected her.

The girl said nothing, so Katie stepped forward and extended her hand. "I'm pleased to meet you." Her hand hung suspended in midair. The girl made no attempt to take it, so she let it fall back to her side, brushing it against her jeans, then shoving it into her pocket.

Cindy pushed the girl down on a bale of straw, then took Katie by the arm and led her several steps away. "I'll be back to get her when I'm done talking to Mark. Keep her entertained."

"Sure," Katie volunteered, looking over her shoulder at the new girl, who stared off into space. She wasn't sure if she would be good company for the kid, but she figured anything would be an improvement over having to spend time with Cindy. "You said we had a lot in common," Katie said to Cindy. "Maybe if you told me what that was, it would help me get to know her."

Cindy looked at her as if she were a fool.

"Well, isn't it obvious?" Cindy spread her arms wide, then dropped them in exasperation.

"She's blind."

← Chapter Three →

Katie stood there dumbfounded. She didn't get the connection.

"Cousin Cindy," the girl said, putting a major emphasis on the word *cousin.* "Is Katie blind too?"

The kid had an excellent set of ears, thought Katie. And what was all this about a cousin? Cindy had never mentioned that the two were related. But now that she studied the younger girl more closely, she saw the family resemblance. Camela had the same pale blond hair and pretty features. But where Cindy's hair was always perfectly clean and carefully styled, Camela's was pulled back into a straggly ponytail and looked as if it could use a good washing. Their eyes were also a different color. Cindy had the same deep blue eyes that the rest of her family had. Camela's eyes were a beautiful shade of sea green. It made for a striking combination with her palomino-colored locks.

Camela sat with her face tilted toward them, waiting for an answer to her question. Cindy didn't bother hiding her irritation. "No, silly. Katie isn't blind. She's got a bum leg."

Both Katie and Camela remained silent, busily trying to

grasp the connection that Cindy was attempting to draw.

Cindy huffed and threw her hands up in exasperation. "A bum leg–you know, as in *handicapped.*"

"Ahhh." Camela nodded her head in perfect understanding. "I see. I'm blind and she can't walk, so that gives us a lot in common..."

The girl's sarcasm was so thick, you could have thrown a horseshoe around it. But the criticism went right over Cindy's head. It was obvious that Camela had a quick wit and didn't care much for her cousin. Katie smiled. The two of them might have something in common after all.

"Well, I better get going," Cindy said. "Mark's supposed to meet me in ten minutes. Don't be a bother to Katie," she warned Camela, then turned to Katie and spoke under her breath. "She specializes in being a bother. Try not to let it get to you. I'm sure you guys will get along fine."

Cindy snickered as she walked back down the shed row. Katie shook her head. The two girls might be from the same family, but they were as different as grass hay and alfalfa. Katie watched Cindy march haughtily away. Her dramatic exit was marred by a stumble that almost landed her in the dirt at her cousin's feet.

"Are you okay, Cousin Cindy?" Camela asked a little too sweetly.

Cindy collected her dignity and glared at Katie, daring her to say something. "You might want to rake this shed row again before somebody breaks their neck." Cindy quickly turned to Camela. "And stop calling me *cousin.* You're my third cousin. That barely makes us related." She turned on her heels and stomped off. Katie considered the satisfied smirk on Camela's face and decided this was going to be an interesting day.

The patter of rain on the barn roof reminded Katie that she had horses to remove from the hotwalker. King craned his neck to look at her and nickered.

"All right, I'm coming, I'm coming." She grabbed the lead rope from the hook on the tack room door. At the sound of movement, Camela turned in her direction. It was growing cooler. The girl might take a chill if she remained seated on the bale of straw in the aisle.

"Would you like to sit in the tack room?" Katie asked. "The heater's on, and it's a lot warmer in there."

"No, thank you. I don't want to be a *bother*. I'll just sit right here until my cousin comes back to get me." Camela shoved her hands into her coat pockets and drew her legs up under her, nestling into the bale of straw.

"You're no bother, Camela. I just don't want you to catch a cold. I think you'd be more comfortable in the tack room."

Camela's only response was to turn her face in the direction of the hotwalker. Katie knew the girl had heard. There was no reason for her not to respond. This must be what Cindy meant when she said the girl could be a pain.

No matter. If Camela wanted to behave like her spoiled cousin, let her. Katie was about to continue with her work when she had a twinge of conscience. The poor kid was in a place she didn't know, escorted around by somebody who wasn't very fond of her, then dumped on someone she didn't know. She was probably just scared.

"Would you like some hot chocolate?" she asked. Camela continued to stare in the direction of the hotwalker. "It's no trouble."

There was still no answer. Okay, Camela could continue to act like her bratty cousin, but it wouldn't stop Katie from trying to be nice to her.

"I've got to get these horses off the walker. Then I'm going to take a short break and make myself a cup of cocoa. I'll make one for you, too. It's really no trouble at all."

Katie thought she saw the corner of the girl's mouth lift in a brief smile, but it quickly vanished. Maybe it had just been her imagination. Camela now wore the same serious look that the stable owner, Tom Ellis, wore when he was watching his colts work. The family resemblance was startling.

It was raining harder. Katie pulled her baseball cap off a peg on the wall and ran to get the horses. They all whinnied, begging to be the first to be put back in a warm, dry stall.

As the only horse in training for the Kentucky Derby, King was the first horse off. Next, Katie snapped the lead on the sweet, blaze-faced filly behind King.

Willow's Destiny, King's two-year-old brother, was the other horse on the hotwalker. Katie still had a few bruises from where he had bucked her off. She let him wait until last.

When all the horses were tucked into their stalls, happily munching on their grass hay, Katie slipped into the tack room to prepare the hot chocolate. Old John, insisted that coffee and a pot of hot water always be kept on hand during the cold months. The damp Oregon winters could chill a person to the bone.

Katie pulled out two mugs that she kept hidden in the back of the leg wrap cabinet. Glasses had a way of walking off and never returning in the stable. Somehow Katie had managed to keep these cups for the past several months. Of course, the drawback to her new hiding place was the dust and horsehair they collected, but that was easy to fix. She pulled out her shirttail and wiped the mugs off, holding them to the light to make sure they were reasonably clean.

Katie then grabbed two packets of cocoa mix. It was the brand with the little marshmallows—her favorite. She poured the hot water and stirred the mixture, breathing in the chocolaty scent. It only needed one more small touch. She reached into the bottom drawer of the coffee stand and pulled out her secret stash of miniature marshmallows, adding even more of the little white puffs to each cup. When they had melted just right, she picked up the mugs and walked over to Camela.

"Here's your cocoa." She set the cup down on the end of the bale. "I'm not sure how you like yours, but I made it with lots of marshmallows. It's right in front of you, okay?"

Camela still didn't speak. Instead, she just turned her face toward Katie.

It felt strange to Katie, having the girl look directly at her and knowing she couldn't see her. Katie expected a simple "Thank you," but the words never came. Camela went back to looking—that was the only way Katie could think to describe it—at the hotwalker.

Katie felt a little hurt that her effort went unappreciated, but she quickly reminded herself that she was doing this for Camela, not for her own satisfaction. She slurped her mug of cocoa noisily, hoping that it might help Camela decide to drink her own. The stubborn girl had to be cold. If she was too pigheaded to sit in the tack room, at least she could swallow the hot drink.

By the time Katie had sucked the last marshmallow from the cup, Camela had still not touched hers. By now, it had to be getting cold. Katie was just about to offer to warm the cocoa when she saw Camela reach for the mug. But instead of picking it up, Camela knocked it from the bale.

Katie's first impression was that the girl had done it on purpose, but she saw the pained expression that flitted across Camela's face before she masked her emotions once again.

Katie picked up Camela's empty mug. "I'm going to get another for you."

She went into the tack room to make another cup, returning with it in a few minutes. Steam rose from the mug as she carried it back to Camela. "Here it is, one foot right in front of you on the edge of the bale. Try again."

To Katie's surprise, the girl reached a tentative hand toward the cup, this time sliding her fingers carefully into the handle and cradling its warmth.

"Thank you," Camela finally said softly, then raised the mug to her lips.

"You're welcome." Katie smiled. Maybe there was hope for the girl after all.

Katie looked at her watch. It was a little after nine. She still had chores to do back at her own house. Jester would be waiting for his morning ride. All that remained to do here was to groom the horses and feed them each a gallon of oats. That was about another thirty minutes' worth of work. She looked at Camela, wondering when Cindy would return. She hoped it would be soon. She didn't want to leave Camela here alone.

Katie picked up the bucket of brushes and entered the first stall. It belonged to Cousin Millie, a three-year-old light bay Thoroughbred. She spoke softly to the lanky filly as she set her brushes down in the straw. Millie paused in her search for a stray oat and turned curious eyes on Katie.

Katie stared into the horse's deep brown eyes, noting the large rim of white that showed at the outer edges. *Wild eyes*, or *devil's eyes*, she had heard trainers call them. They believed these horses were unpredictable. John said it was an old superstition.

Come to think of it, Millie wasn't exactly the most easygoing horse in the barn. So far, Katie was the only person at the farm that Millie hadn't kicked. The filly was as handy with her back feet as any Olympic soccer player. Katie wasn't sure why she had escaped Millie's escapades, but she was thankful that she had.

She snapped the lead on the filly's halter and tied her to the ring on the wall. Most of Willow Run's horses would just stand in the middle of the stall enjoying the grooming, but Millie was a wiggle-wart. And if there was one thing Katie had learned over the years, it was never to take chances where these big animals were concerned.

No matter how intelligent she thought a horse was, she kept in mind a saying of old John's. *"Remember that this is a twelve-hundred-pound animal controlled by a brain the size of an orange."* That vivid image always came back to her when one of her charges did something that didn't make any sense.

Katie grabbed the hoof pick and started on Millie's front left hoof, working her way around to the other side. When she finished brushing the filly, she moved on to the gelding in the next stall. King was the last one that needed to be done. Katie looked at her watch, then at Camela. What was keeping Cindy? Then she remembered that Cindy was with the new jockey.

Katie imagined Cindy tossing her braid over her shoulder as she laughed and showed off her expensive new show saddle to Mark. Katie grimaced but then pushed the thought aside. There was no reason to be bothered by Mark and Cindy's becoming friends. By now, Cindy was probably begging him to help her get her gallop license.

Katie smiled to herself. If he could teach Cindy enough to get her licensed, he must be one great jockey. Maybe he could help her too. She almost laughed aloud. If Cindy was bent on being a gallop girl, Mark had his work cut out for him. The poor guy would be so busy, he wouldn't have any time left to help Katie.

She peeked around the corner of the stall. Camela was still sitting in the same spot with a very bored look on her face. If Cindy didn't return soon, Katie decided, she would walk Camela up to the house before she left for home.

Katie decided to brush King in the shed row so she could keep Camela company. Just because the girl didn't want to talk didn't mean Katie couldn't speak to her. She warned Camela that she would be moving a horse into the aisle, noting a slight look of alarm on Camela's face. Then she pulled King from his stall and hooked the cross-ties to his halter.

"Camela, this is Willow King," Katie said as she picked up his front hoof and cleaned out the dirt and small rocks. "He's in training for the Kentucky Derby. Did you know we had a horse being prepped for the Run for the Roses?"

Camela still didn't say a word, but she had her head cocked, listening, so Katie decided to give her a short history of Willow King's life.

"King is my horse now, but he was born on this farm. He's out of Mr. Ellis's stakes mare Gray Dancer. They had high hopes pinned on this colt. He was out of this farm's best mare and sired by Willow Run's prize stallion. You can imagine how disappointed everyone was when the colt was born with really crooked legs."

Katie picked up the rubber currycomb and went to work on the dried saddle marks on King's back. The colt swished his tail and gnashed his teeth as if he wanted her to stop, but Katie knew he was playing. King loved to be brushed. If she were to stop, he would look at her with those big brown eyes and nudge her to get started again.

"Anyway," Katie continued, "Mr. Ellis had called the veterinarian to have the colt put down. I couldn't stand it. He was so perfect in every other way. John, Willow Run's trainer, said he thought King's legs might straighten enough that he would be of some use as a riding horse, but Mr. Ellis didn't want anyone to know that a crooked-legged colt had come from his prize stallion.

"So we struck a deal. I had to lease my show horse, Jester, to Cindy for two years, and I had to work off King's vet bills. We had to ship King and his mother to my house, and I wasn't allowed to tell a single soul that King was from Willow Run Farm."

Katie picked up the stiff brush and used quick, even strokes to remove the remainder of the dirt from King's coat. "We considered putting casts on King's legs, but John's remedy of sunshine and plenty of green pasture to run in turned out to be exactly what this colt needed. His legs are now perfectly straight, and he's getting ready to win the Kentucky Derby. Now, of course, Mr. Ellis wants *everyone* to know that King is from Willow Run Farm."

She tossed the brush she was using into the box and grabbed the one with the soft bristles to finish off his coat. "I just wish I could be the one to ride him in the Derby."

Why had she just said that? Katie immediately looked at Camela to see if she had heard. The girl's expression never wavered. *Oh, what's the difference,* she thought. *Camela doesn't seem to talk much anyway. What could it hurt?* After all, Katie wanted to talk about it.

"I know it's crazy, Camela, but I want to get my jockey's license. I've been galloping for a year now. My mom's the only one who knows about this." She paused, then added, "And now you know too. I don't want to tell anyone else, because, well, what if I can't do it? This stupid leg of mine makes everything harder. I don't want to see the look of pity on everyone's face if I fail. Sometimes I wonder if I should even bother trying."

Katie could see that Camela was listening with interest. She smiled. Maybe the two of them could become friends. She unsnapped King from the cross-ties.

"Would you like to pet Willow King?" Katie asked as she moved the colt toward the young girl, stopping when she saw Camela shrink away. "He's gentle for a stallion."

Camela didn't say a word, but she shook her head vigorously, moving farther away toward the outer edge of the bale.

Willow King lowered his head, his nostrils blowing softly as he extended his muzzle curiously toward Camela.

"He wants to meet you," Katie said. "His nose is at the end of the bale if you'd like to reach your hand up to pet him."

At first Camela sat frozen to the spot, but after a moment, she cautiously lifted her open hand toward the big colt's muzzle. King gently nuzzled the young girl's soft palm, and Camela let out a small shriek and immediately pulled her hand back, burying it deep in her pocket.

King's head popped up, and Katie laughed. "I think you just startled each other."

A small smile started at the corners of Camela's mouth, then quickly disappeared at the sound of footsteps tromping up the aisle.

"Yoo-hoo, I'm back. I hope I didn't keep you waiting too long." Cindy stopped in her tracks when she saw Camela and Katie standing there with Willow King. "What are you doing?" Cindy placed her hands on her hips as she looked from one to the other.

"Camela was making friends with King," Katie answered, not understanding why Cindy was so upset.

Cindy turned to her young cousin. "I said you could come down to the barn because you were bored, but you shouldn't get close to the horses. Not after everything you've been through."

Katie furrowed her brow. "What do you mean? Why bring Camela down to the barn if she can't pet the horses?"

"Stay out of things that aren't your business," Cindy warned as she helped Camela off the bale. Then she quickly switched the topic, presenting them with one of her sugary-sweet smiles. "Sorry I'm late, but Mark and I were having so much fun that I lost track of the time. He really is a great rider. And he's going to make me one too. You better watch yourself, Katie Durham, or I'll be stealing your mounts right out from under you."

Cindy grabbed Camela's hand and dragged her down the aisle. "Let's hurry. I've got to do my nails for school tomorrow. We're having a big pep rally after fifth period. Mark's going to be there, and I want to look my best."

Camela wrestled her arm from her cousin's grasp and turned to face Katie. "My Irish granddaddy used to say, '*You'll never plow a field by turning it over in your mind.*'" With that said, she looped her arm around Cindy's and allowed herself to be dragged back down the shed row.

"Whatever that means," Cindy called back over her shoulder. "She's a strange girl. Don't pay any attention to her."

Katie smiled. She knew exactly what Camela meant. She was telling her to stop procrastinating and follow her dream of becoming a jockey.

✈ Chapter Four ✈

Katie had a difficult time concentrating on her schoolwork because today was the day she would get to ride King again. She glanced at the clock on the wall above her teacher's head. It hadn't moved a bit since the last time she looked.

She heard Mr. Lees lecture on one of her favorite books, but the words went in one ear and out the other. For a good student, she was having a very hard time keeping up with what was being said. She looked down at her paper. She hadn't written any notes. Instead, there was a stick-figure rendition of her and King leaping out of the starting gate at Churchill Downs.

She tapped her pencil on the desk and sneaked another peek at the clock. Only two more hours until she could get back to the barn.

During the school week in the winter, Willow Run Farm used a divided schedule. Since many of the grooms and exercise riders were students, half the horses were worked in the morning, the other half in the afternoon. On the days when the track was too frozen to use in the early hours, all the horses would be galloped after school let out.

Katie began to think about what Camela had said to her yesterday. The kid was right. She would never get her jockey's license just by *thinking* about it. She had to take action.

Katie bit down on the end of her pencil. She had a tough decision to make. She was ready to get started on her jockey's license, but she still didn't want to tell anyone about it. After some deep thought, she decided to keep her mouth closed for a little while longer—at least until she had the courage to approach Mark about lessons. In the meantime, she could practice in secret. It wouldn't hurt anyone.

A twinge of guilt pricked her conscience. Jason had been there for her since the beginning of her racetrack career. Of all people, he should know about her new venture. He would be proud of her and tell her to go for it. But what would he think if she didn't make it? After all he'd done for her, she'd hate to let him down.

Katie pushed the thought aside. She would tell him later…maybe.

The bell for next period sounded. Katie gathered her books and shoved them into her backpack. She joined the crush of students crowding the hallway, shuffling through the narrow passage like a herd of cattle.

"Katie!" Jan squeezed through the crowd, finding her way to Katie's side. "Have you seen Mark yet?"

"No, but I haven't exactly been looking for him." That was a half-truth. She had kept her eyes open at lunchtime, hoping to see him in the cafeteria. But when Jason had joined her, she stopped searching.

Jan shifted her books to her other arm. "I passed him in the hall and I hardly recognized him. He looked out of place without his helmet and riding boots. But he's still *really* cute. All the girls are talking to him. He recognized me and said hello, so I guess his head isn't too big yet." She laughed. "But who knows, after he wins the Kentucky Derby on Willow King, he'll probably be too cool to talk to anyone."

Katie scrunched her lips together and tried to act as if the statement didn't bother her, but Jan could tell that it did.

"What's the matter, Katie?" Jan asked. "You've got a horse that will probably run in the Derby and a really good jockey who can get him there. Did you know Mark was the second leading rider at Aqueduct last season?"

Katie took a deep breath. If she couldn't tell her best friend, who *could* she tell? "Jan…*I* want to be the jockey who's on Willow King when he goes to the Kentucky Derby."

Jan stopped in her tracks, her mouth working like that of a goldfish in a glass bowl. When no words came out, she snapped her jaw shut. Then a big smile spread slowly across her face. She grabbed Katie and pulled her into the nearest doorway.

"Katie Durham, of all the crazy things you've done in your life, this one beats them all. I love it! I can't wait to tell everybody. Especially little Miss Cindy Ellis. Won't she be purple with envy!"

"Wait!" Katie instantly remembered why she'd wanted to keep this a secret. Taking Jan by the arm, Katie looked her friend straight in the eye. "This has got to stay between you and me. I don't want *anyone* to know."

Jan rolled her eyes and let out an exaggerated sigh. "Katie, this is one of the greatest things you've ever done. Very few women have ever ridden in the Kentucky Derby, and no female jockey has ever won it. You could be the first!"

"But I haven't done it yet," Katie protested. "What if I'm not good enough? I don't want to let everyone down."

Katie dropped her arms and stared at the cream-colored tile of the hall floor. A large piece of gum with a shoe print in it caught her attention. That was what she thought she would be if everyone knew she had tried this and failed—a squished piece of bubblegum. And the shoe print would be Cindy's.

Jan grabbed Katie's hand and squeezed it. "Katie, I've known you all my life. In all this time, the only person you've ever let down is yourself; and that's because your expectations are so high. You can do this. I know you can. But if you want to keep it a secret, I'll keep my big mouth shut."

Katie smiled. "I wish I had as much faith in myself as you do. Thanks, Jan."

Jan dragged them back out into the meandering current of students. "No problem! But are you sure I can't even tell one person? Not even Jason?"

"Especially not Jason." Katie's conscience pricked her again. "I do plan to tell him, though," she assured Jan. "I just want to wait a little longer."

"I understand," Jan said.

The two-minute warning bell sounded. Katie stopped outside room twelve. "I'll see you on the bus."

Later that day, Katie sat on one of the old chairs in the tack room and pulled on her riding boots. They weren't the expensive kind Cindy had, but they were good enough to get the job done. If she took good care of them, they would last another year.

She stood and stretched. Her back still bothered her a bit, but it was healed enough to ride. As long as King didn't pull on her too strongly, she'd be okay.

Jason's truck pulled up to the barn, and Katie went out to greet him. The gray clouds hung low in the sky and threatened rain, but it would be a while before they had any precipitation. Katie pushed her riding helmet on and walked to the end of the barn.

"We can get at least five horses out before it starts to rain," she said. "John's working with the young horses at the upper barn. He left a list of what he wanted done. I can tack King, and we can get him out first while the track is still good."

"Uh...Kat." Jason looked at the ground, avoiding her eyes as he spoke.

Katie didn't like the look on Jason's face. It appeared as if he had eaten something that disagreed with him. It was the same look he'd had several months ago when he came to tell her that one of her favorite colts had been seriously injured and had to be put down. She knew she wasn't going to like what he had to say.

"What's up, Jason?"

He scuffed at the dirt with the toe of his boot and jammed his hands deep into his pockets. "I saw Mark at school today. We were talking over lunch. It looks like Tom Ellis is going to use him on all his stock, and since King's regular jockey broke his leg in that accident a few weeks ago, Mark will probably be riding King too. Maybe as early as Wednesday's race."

"And…?"

Jason finally looked her in the eye. He drew a deep breath. "Look, Katie, I know how much you've enjoyed exercising King, but Mr. Ellis said that if Mark is going to ride the colt in the races, he might as well be galloping him from now on so they can get used to each other. And John agrees."

Katie's shoulders slumped and she breathed a defeated sigh. She felt as if someone had just slugged her in the stomach. Although she knew there was nothing he could do about it, she somehow felt that Jason had betrayed her.

"So that's it?" She took off her helmet and brushed the hair out of her eyes. "I don't get a say in any of this? He's *my horse.*" Katie bit her lip. She would not cry. She *would not* cry.

Jason put his arm around her shoulders. "Of course you have a say in this. But I also know you will do what's *best* for King. We've got the Jim Beam Stakes coming up in three weeks and a couple of big races in California. You know how important the Jim Beam is. King has got to get used to his rider."

"I know, I know. The Jim Beam is one of the richest Derby prep races, and it's a good predictor of Triple Crown talent," she said mimicking Tom Ellis's lecture.

Katie pursed her lips. She knew that Jason was on her side. And she knew that Mark would need to ride King if he were going to be his official jockey. Since it would take a while for Katie to get her license, Mark would probably have to ride King in a few races anyway. But it still didn't ease the ache she felt.

Maybe she was crazy for wanting to be a jockey. Not

only was racing a dangerous sport, but a jockey was always in the public eye. Racegoers and horse owners were constantly scrutinizing each race, looking for the reason their horses lost. They usually blamed the jockeys. Did she really want to deal with that kind of pressure?

And what about the fact that the most famous horse race in the world, the Kentucky Derby, could be one of her first races? She felt queasy just thinking about it.

She looked up at Jason. Concern was etched in his face. He knew how much she loved to ride King. He just didn't know that she wanted to be a jockey. Neither did old John. They were doing what they thought was best for King.

"You're right," Katie conceded. "It's just that I was looking forward to this the whole week. It's kind of a letdown."

Jason placed her riding helmet back on her head. "Don't forget we've got all these other horses to go. That'll keep your mind off King for a while. I can even saddle up ol' Willow's Destiny if you want to have another shot at the national saddle bronc finals."

"No rodeo for me, thank you," Katie declined. "I have no desire to eat dirt soup again anytime soon. I know Willow's Destiny is a full brother to my horse, but someone must have switched foals at birth," she joked. "That colt's nothing like Willow King."

Katie grabbed the equipment from the tack room, placing it on the stall door of Dream Catcher, a six-year-old mare that was doing very well for the stable. "So when is Mark coming for King?"

Jason looked at his watch. "He should be here by now. I'll saddle King, then take you out to the track on Dream Catcher. Mark'll be here by the time I get back."

"Anyone home?" Cindy marched up the shed row dragging her cousin behind her. Camela's cane tapped a rapid tattoo up the aisle as she tried to remain upright in their headlong race to the tack room.

Cindy plunked her down on the same bale of straw she had rested upon the day before, ordering her to *stay put.*

"Lord knows why, but she asked to come back down here today. I guess you two must have hit it off. Camela doesn't like anybody, but she seems to be able to tolerate your company, so I guess you get to baby-sit again."

Katie saw a look of hurt pass quickly across the younger girl's face. "Camela is hardly a baby, Cindy. And yes, we hit it off just fine. Camela knows she's more than welcome to visit here anytime she wants."

"Good," Cindy countered, "because I plan on leaving her here a lot. She gets under my feet, and she's no fun at all. You can deal with her stubborn ways."

Katie was amazed that Cindy would speak like this right in front of Camela. The girl was blind, but she certainly wasn't deaf. She had proved that yesterday. The kid had ears like a satellite dish.

Cindy spotted Jason coming out of King's stall. "Mark tells me he's going to ride King again today."

Jason set his jaw, giving Cindy a look that warned her not to start anything. "Yes, he should be here any moment," Jason said.

"Is that so?" Cindy flipped her braid over her shoulder and stared at Katie. "Still, it's got to be hard on you. King is *your horse,* and I know how much you were looking forward to exercising him today."

Katie finished tacking the mare and stepped outside the

stall, giving Jason a smile of appreciation. "You're right," she said to Cindy. "King is my horse, and I can ride him anytime I want. But this is your father's training farm, and John is the trainer here. They want to do what's *best* for Willow King, and so do I. Since Mark will be riding King in his next race, it's best if they have a chance to get used to each other."

Katie smiled as she saw the smart-aleck grin fade from Cindy's lips. She knew how much Cindy hated it when her goading didn't work.

Jason stepped into the aisle. "Katie, we've got to get busy here. It's going to rain soon. Cindy, we'll look after your cousin. Go on with your business."

Cindy gave Jason her best smile. Katie had the feeling that if she turned her back, the little flirt would try to steal Jason from her.

Cindy turned and strode up the shed row. Katie heard a soft thud and looked up to see the haughty girl sprawled in the dirt by Camela's feet. She rose and brushed the dirt from her tan riding breeches with quick, angry strokes.

"I told you to fix this shed row," Cindy grouched. "See that it's done by tomorrow or I'll tell my father."

Katie didn't miss the look of satisfaction on Camela's petite face. The girl was almost gloating.

"Camela," Katie called. "There are going to be a lot of horses going up and down these aisles. You need to sit where you won't get stepped on. I think the feed shed will be a good place. There's a platform there where we can place a chair, and you'll have the perfect spot to keep track of all that's happening. Is that okay?"

There was no answer. Katie had hoped for one but

didn't really expect it.

"What's with her?" Jason asked. "She can hear, can't she?"

"Of course she can. She just doesn't like to talk much."

Jason shrugged his shoulders, then let out a small chuckle. "Are you sure she's related to Cindy?"

Katie saw a rare smile on Camela's face. She knew, in that moment, that Jason had been approved.

"You get the chair, and I'll get Camela," she said.

After Katie had reseated Camela without a single word falling from the young girl's lips, she grabbed the mare and headed to the end of the barn to wait for a leg up. When she passed the spot where Cindy had fallen, she inspected the area. Except for the indentations where Cindy had hit the ground, she couldn't find anything that would cause a fall.

Katie shook her head as she eased the mare forward. Maybe Cindy was just getting clumsy.

⇥ *Chapter Five* ⇤

Katie backtracked Dream Catcher on the outside rail at a walk. When the way was clear, she turned the mare and trotted down the middle of the track, grabbing a low cross on the reins as she posted to the rhythm of the horse's gait. When she felt the mare was warmed up, Katie smooched her into a gallop, leaning forward to balance her hands in front of the withers. She stayed in the center of the raceway, as the inside rail was reserved for fast works only. She remembered an accident caused by a beginner who was slow-galloping his horses on the rail when two breezing horses came flying around a turn. It wasn't a pretty sight.

These were just some of the rules she'd had to learn in order to get her gallop license. Now she needed to find someone who could teach her all the rules for getting a jockey's license. There were a few older jockeys who rode for Willow Run Farm, but Katie knew she'd feel more comfortable with someone her own age. She thought again about Mark. He would be a good teacher, but she wasn't sure she'd have the nerve to ask his help. After all, Mark might lose his chance to ride a Derby horse if he taught her.

Another horse pounded through on the inside rail. His ears were pinned in challenge, and his nostrils flared as he drew abreast of them. In a flash, he sprinted past with his tail flying, kicking up sand as he went.

Dream Catcher caught the excitement and wanted to go after the horse. Katie pulled in several more inches of rein, bowing the mare's neck and holding her steady. The wind blew in her face as a thousand pounds of muscle and spirit galloped down the track beneath her. It felt like riding a powder keg through a corridor of flames—she never knew when the powder would ignite and the horse would explode.

They finished the gallop, and Katie looked over her shoulder, making sure the track was clear before she moved to the outside and pulled up. Jason had another horse tacked and waiting for her at the exit gate.

By the time she finished the last horse, Mark still hadn't shown. "Are you sure he knows he was supposed to ride King today?" Katie asked as she pulled the saddle from her mount's back. If Mark proved to be undependable, maybe it would be a mistake to let him race King this week.

Jason removed the bridle and dipped the bit in the nearest bucket of water to clean it off. "I just talked with him a couple of hours ago. He said he'd be here by four o'clock at the latest."

Katie looked at her watch. It was four-fifteen. She turned to Camela, who was still seated on the deck of the feed shed. "Camela, did anyone come by while we were out at the track?"

Camela continued just to sit there, acting as if she hadn't heard a word. Katie was beginning to get tired of

Camela's game. She raised her face to the sky and silently prayed for the patience needed to handle the girl. A raindrop suddenly landed on her cheek and rolled down her face. The clouds had quickly turned dark and hung lower in the sky. It wouldn't be much longer before a downpour.

"You better move a little farther under the overhang," she warned Camela. "It looks like the rain's coming."

Camela didn't move an inch.

Jason glanced at his watch, then removed his black Stetson and scratched his head. "I don't know what happened to Mark, but we can't wait any longer. We've got to get a good gallop into King now so he's right for Wednesday night. It looks like it's going to be a real soaker, and John would have my hide if he knew I was galloping King in the rain when I didn't have to. So let's do it now."

Jason smiled at Katie. "Looks like you're getting your wish today. I assume you won't mind galloping him."

Katie couldn't keep the smile off her face. "Let me get something for Camela, and I'll be right there."

She prepared some cocoa, throwing in an extra bunch of marshmallows, then walked it out to Camela. "Here's another cup of hot chocolate. Since you're going to be sitting out in the rain, you'll need the extra warmth. I'll set it right here on this barrel." She made as much noise as possible when she put the cup down so Camela would have no doubt where it was.

"Let's go," Jason yelled as he moved King into the shed row. "We've got about ten minutes to spare. I want to be back in the barn before the rain gets heavy."

Katie ran up the aisle. Jason gave her a leg up, then led King down the shed row while Katie adjusted her equipment. "Be careful by the hay pile," she warned. "There's a rut somewhere that Cindy keeps tripping over."

Katie heard a giggle and looked over her shoulder to see Camela sitting there with a mischievous grin on her face. Something had tickled the girl's funny bone.

Mark was running down the shed row calling for Jason and Katie. When no one answered, he tried for John and Tom Ellis. He saw King's empty stall and let out a disgusted sigh. "Dang!"

He heard the creaking of a chair and turned to see a blond girl plunk a cup down on a barrel. "Hi." Mark walked over to where she sat. "Do you know where everyone's at?"

Mark was perplexed when the kid didn't say a word. She didn't even acknowledge him.

"Hel-looo." Mark brought his face down level with the girl's. He noticed her vacant stare but didn't trust his own judgment, so he waved his hand in front of her face. "Can you hear me?" Mark asked as he passed his hand one more time in front of Camela's eyes. There was still no response.

"Great!" he grouched. "Somebody's run off with my Derby winner and you can't even tell me who it was!" He cracked his whip across his shiny black boots. "I knew I shouldn't have stopped to talk to Cindy. Now she's made me miss my mount."

"Oh, well," Mark scoffed, "if another jockey has stolen my horse, I'm sure I can butter up Cindy enough to sweet-talk her father into putting me back on him." He laughed. "I just hope it's Katie riding King today." He continued speaking even though he wasn't sure if the girl could hear him. "I don't have to worry about her. She's *no* competition.

I better get out to the track and have a look for myself."

Mark stepped off the feed shed deck and caught his boot on something. He hit the ground with a thump, then quickly picked himself up, muttering as he dusted the dirt off his knees. He looked at the girl, then turned on his heel and went to find Willow King.

John was standing with Jason at the rail when Mark arrived. The old trainer waved him over. "We missed you this afternoon, son."

Mark stepped up to the rail and cleared his throat. "I'm sorry, sir. I got held up at school. It took me longer than I thought."

"That's okay. Katie girl's riding King today. Her and that colt get along just fine." John turned his attention back to the track as Willow King passed the mile marker on his two-mile gallop. "That girl sure knows how to handle a horse."

Mark watched Katie take King around the bend. He was surprised at her skill. She leaned into the turn with the horse and kept the reins just tight enough to keep him at a steady pace and support his balance. *It's a good thing she doesn't have her jockey's license or I'd be out of a job,* Mark thought. But all he said to John was, "Yeah, she's not too bad, I guess."

By the time they got King back to the barn, the rain had turned to a steady drizzle. Mark followed John and Jason. He promised to stop by after school the next day to breeze King for six furlongs. Then he made his way to Katie and helped her remove the tack and place the cool-out blanket on King. The weather was too wet to put him on the hot-walker. He would have to be hand-walked, as in the old days.

"You did a real fine job with King today," Mark complimented her.

"Thanks. I really like riding him. He and I have a sort of special friendship. It's fun to ride King because it feels like he's got all this energy stored up inside him and he's just waiting for me to ask him to use it."

Mark looked confused by Katie's reference to a special friendship, but he let it pass. "Well, I can see why he's training for the Derby. He's got real speed."

Mark patted King's neck. A good horse was a good horse as far as he was concerned. A good jockey could get what he wanted from any horse, and he intended to be the one to get the best out of Willow King. He finished hooking the blanket, then gave Katie his best smile as he handed her the lead rope. "And, Katie, I really like riding him too. Thanks for giving me a shot to prove myself Wednesday night. I plan to be the best rider at Portland Downs this season. You won't be sorry. I'm going to win that race for you."

"With all that confidence, let's hope you don't blow it," Katie teased. They laughed together, and Jason turned to look. He frowned, then went about putting away the equipment. A funny pit formed in Katie's stomach, but she ignored it. She wasn't doing anything wrong.

"Are you busy tonight?" Mark asked.

"I've got homework to do."

"There's a few of us going out for pizza. Would you like to join us?"

Katie fidgeted with King's blanket. When she looked back at Jason, he was staring directly at her with a questioning look on his face. She quickly dropped her gaze and smiled nervously at Mark. "Thanks, but I'm not allowed to go out on a school night. My mom's pretty strict about that."

Mark tried another angle. "What about your dad? Maybe he'll say yes?"

Katie scratched King behind the ears. "My father passed away when I was eight. My mom's the final word in our house."

Mark was silent for a moment. "Sorry, I just figured you might like to go. Cindy will be there."

Katie nearly rolled her eyes. If Cindy was going, then she definitely wouldn't be. Who wanted to spend an evening listening to Cindy brag about her new clothes and expensive saddles?

"Well, maybe another time." Mark patted King and straightened his forelock. "I better get going. I've still got to give Cindy a gallop lesson. It's a good thing they've got a covered arena here."

"I don't envy you your job," Katie said. "I had to give Cindy equitation lessons for the show ring this past summer. She's kind of hard to work with."

"She's a little knot-headed," Mark agreed. "But we'll get her out on the big track pretty soon."

Katie said good-bye to Mark, then muttered, "Heaven help us all."

Jason excused himself as he stepped past Camela's chair and reached for an armload of hay from the feed shed. "What did Mark want?" he asked Katie. He was trying to sound aloof, but Katie knew he suspected that something was up between her and Mark. "He just wanted to talk about King's race. He's trying to sell me on the idea that he's the best jockey for Willow King." She rearranged the horse's blanket, looking everywhere but at Jason. If there was nothing going on, why had she lied to him? Mark had only asked her out for pizza, and Cindy was going to be there too. It wasn't as if he had asked her on a date or anything.

"I'll be leaving in a minute. You like a ride home?" Jason took hold of King's halter, rubbing the deep groove under the horse's jawbone. Katie paused for a moment and then finally got up the nerve to look at him. "Thanks, but it'll take at least twenty minutes to walk this horse dry."

The rain pounded on the roof with the intensity of a herd of horses turning down the homestretch. Jason pulled his collar up and his hat low over his eyes. "I'll run up to the top barn and check on the brood mares. We've got a couple of them due to foal any day now. I'll be back in twenty minutes. If Camela is still here, we'll drop her by the big house on the way to take you home."

Katie smiled. What would she do without Jason? He was always so kind and thoughtful. Most of the girls at school would love to have him for their boyfriend—including Cindy. She should drop this fascination with Mark. It would only lead to trouble.

She turned to Jason and nodded. "Okay. I'll be ready in twenty minutes. Thanks."

Katie coiled the lead rope in her hand and walked King down the shed row. When she passed the feed room, she noticed that Camela quickly moved her chair farther into the shed as if she feared getting kicked or stepped on.

"It's okay, it's King. Remember, he's very gentle. He won't hurt you," she assured the girl. But Camela stayed where she was. Katie continued down the aisle, making several passes up and back before she stopped to give King a drink of water. He sank his nose in up to the nostrils, sucking greedily at the cool liquid. "Easy, buddy, we don't need you getting a bellyache." She pulled his head from the bucket and headed back down the aisle.

Katie watered King several more times. She ran her hand down his muscled chest, checking to see if he was still hot. When King finally refused the water and was cool to the touch, she tied him in the cross-ties next to the feed shed and fetched the brush box.

As Katie worked the dried sweat out of his coat, she marveled at how far they had come. She threw her arms around King's neck. "I hope I'm aboard you when the gate opens at Churchill Downs on that first Saturday in May. We'll make a great team." King bobbed his head and blew through his lips. Katie laughed. "You think so too, don't you, boy?"

Katie finished with the soft brush. "I better get to work on my jockey's license or you'll be going to Kentucky without me. I've just got to get up my nerve to ask Mark. He's got a lot of ambition. Maybe if I promise him a couple of races on you, he'll agree to teach me how to be a jockey."

Camela coughed and edged her seat closer to the entryway of the feed room. Katie had forgotten she was there.

"I suppose you think I'm crazy for talking to a horse, but I do it all the time," she said. "He likes the sound of my voice, and I like having someone to talk to." She looked at her watch. Jason would be there soon. "Camela, I like to talk to you too. But I'll also listen if you ever want to say anything."

Katie put King in his stall, then closed the tack shed and returned to where Camela sat. She hunkered down beside the girl. "Do you think I should ask Mark to help me get my jockey's license? He was a top rider at one of the biggest tracks in the country. And besides, he's really cute and all the girls at school are trying to get his attention."

Camela snorted and averted her face.

"You don't think he's a good choice?" she asked, incredulous. Did the kid have something against him, or was it just her general dislike of the entire population? Katie wondered.

Jason pulled up in his truck and laid on the horn. "Come on, you two."

Camela picked up her white cane and took hold of Katie's arm. They made their way down the aisle with the cane beating a rapid rhythm on the packed dirt and barn walls.

"Be careful when we get to the end here," Katie warned. "There's a rough spot somewhere that people keep tripping on."

Camela pursed her lips together, but Katie could see a hint of a smile peeking out at the edges. Would she ever be able to figure this girl out?

Jason jumped out of his pickup and ran around to grab Camela, helping her gently into the truck. They drove to the Ellis house with only the scratchy sound of a country song playing on the vehicle's worn-out radio.

When they arrived, Jason told Katie to wait in the car while he took Camela to the door. He removed his jacket and held it over the girl's head so she wouldn't get wet. Camela paused for a moment outside the truck and turned to Katie. "My grandfather once said, *'Never mistake a goat's beard for a fine stallion's tail.'*" And with that, she turned and trotted up the walk with Jason.

Katie stared after her. Camela had struck with her riddles once again. This time Katie wasn't so sure what the message meant, but she was sure it had something to do with Mark.

On Wednesday afternoon, Katie and Jan jumped off the school bus and ran up the driveway to Katie's house. Jason would be there to pick them up in fifteen minutes. Old John had taken King to Portland Downs early that morning. He liked to give the horses plenty of time to settle down and rest up before a race.

"I've got everything ready to go," Katie's mother shouted after her as Katie ran down the hall, pulling off her shoes and jacket as she went.

"Calm down, Katie. This is an easy race," Jan said as she handed Katie some clean jeans. "The Jim Beam is three weeks away. *That's* the one you need to be nervous about. This is just a warm-up race."

"I know, I know." Katie stuffed her right leg into her jeans and almost lost her balance. In a couple of hours she would get to see King race. No matter how many times she watched the colt run, she always felt the same excitement.

"Jason's here," her mother called as Katie finished changing out of her school clothes. "Let's go."

Fitting everybody into Jason's pickup was a tight squeeze. Katie listened to everyone's excited chatter, but she didn't feel much like talking. She was too busy worrying about the race.

This would be Mark's first race on Willow King, and it wouldn't be easy. A cold front had moved into the area, making the already poor footing of the track even worse. John had considered scratching King from the race, but Tom Ellis had insisted they keep him in. There wasn't another race available before the Jim Beam, and King needed the speed work.

When they arrived at Portland Downs, Katie went directly to King's stall while the rest of the gang met John at the diner for a quick supper before the races.

"Are you sure you don't want me to bring you something?" Jason offered Katie.

"I'm sure—you know me, I can't eat a bite until it's all over. Maybe later," said Katie with a nervous smile.

Jason squeezed her hand. "You better get a grip on yourself. If you're this worked up over a small-stakes race, you'll need a straitjacket for the Derby. Don't cha think that'll look kind of funny in the win photo?"

"You're right," Katie said as she took a deep, calming breath. "It's just a race, and anything can happen in a horse race."

"That-a-girl." Jason playfully slugged Katie's shoulder.

"I'll save the real worrying for the Jim Beam and the Derby," Katie teased.

Jason gave her hair a playful tug, then left to find the others. Katie went over to King's stall and busied herself by grooming him. She talked gently to him the entire time. She could hear the tractors as they ran over the track with their big disks, breaking up the frozen dirt.

When the call came for the first race, Katie decided to watch a couple of races to see how the horses were faring.

If there were any breakdowns due to the track's condition, she would scratch King. She didn't care what Mr. Ellis would say. He had agreed to take King into his racing stable for twenty-five percent of the win purse, but if King broke down, he would get nothing. That was an equation Katie knew Mr. Ellis would definitely understand.

The first four races went off with no troubles, but Katie could hear the hardness of the ground as the horses thundered past. She shoved her mittened hands deep into her pockets and watched the patterns her breath made in the cold air. It was time to get King ready for his race.

When she got back to the barn, John was checking King's racing bridle. "Here," he said, handing the bridle to Katie. "Put this inside your jacket and keep the bit warm for King."

The feel of the cold steel against her body was enough to make her gasp, but better *she* suffer the cold than her horse. On a night like this, he'd need all the extra comfort he could get.

Thirty minutes later, they were on their way to the paddock for the feature race.

"Has anyone seen Mark?" Katie asked.

"I hear he's decided to pull off King and ride another colt," John said as he winked at Jason from his seat on the pony-horse.

Katie halted in her tracks, her heart skidding to a stop. It wasn't until she heard everyone laughing that she realized the trainer was joking. She scowled at John. "That's not very funny." When they all laughed again, she decided to join them. "Okay, I get the hint. I'll lighten up."

When they reached the paddock, Katie took King's

reins from the trainer and led him into the saddling stall. She heard all the *ooh*s and *ahh*s as she led King back out for a few rounds before the jockeys mounted up.

Katie smiled nervously at Mark when he finally arrived. "Are you sick?" he inquired.

"No, she just gets a little of those pre-race jitters," John said.

Mark flashed her a winning grin. "This is going to be a ride in the park, Katie. You can wait for us in the winner's circle."

"The track's pretty rough," John said. "Don't push this colt. If he can win it on his own, let him. I want him to have plenty left for the Jim Beam. We don't need him getting hurt." The trainer left to mount up on the pony-horse, leaving Jason to give the rider a leg up.

Katie and Jan ran to get a place on the rail. As cold as it was, they didn't have to fight for a good spot. Everyone else, including Katie's mother, was up in the clubhouse. The girls blew warm breaths into their mittens and waited for the race to start.

"The horses are at the gate," the announcer called just as Jason joined them at the rail. *"Willow King is the first to be loaded."*

Katie held her breath, praying that King would stay calm and focused. The longer a horse sat in the gate, the more likely it was to cause trouble and get a late start. This was only a six-furlong race; King couldn't afford a bad start.

"They're all in," the loudspeaker announced. *"And they're off!"*

Katie stood on her toes, looking for Mark's red racing silks. "Where is he?"

"Oh, my gosh, there." Jan pointed.

Katie couldn't believe her eyes and ears. The sound of a single gate popping open echoed across the infield as she saw King charge out of the gate a full second behind the other horses.

"What happened?"

Jan shook her head. "It looks like his gate didn't open. He's almost twenty lengths behind the other horses."

"Bold Order has the lead, and Connie's Hope is running up to challenge. Willow King is in the rear with a lot of daylight between him and the next horse."

"I don't believe it," Katie cried. "How could that happen? Come on, King! Run!" From where she stood, Katie could see King shaking his head, trying to grab the bit and catch the pack, but Mark kept a death grip on him, pulling the colt out to the center of the racecourse.

"What's he doing?" She turned to Jason. "Why won't he let him run?" She watched in misery as Mark stood in the irons and breezed King well behind the other horses.

"And it's Connie's Hope by three lengths at the wire, with Rags to Riches second and Bold Order third. Willow King is the last to cross the line."

Katie expelled a defeated breath, watching it form a cloud in the cold air. "I thought Mark was a good jockey. He didn't even try to catch the other horses." She felt Jason's hand on her shoulder and turned to look into his blue eyes, searching for an answer. "Did you see that?"

"It's not his fault, Kat," Jason said. "Mark did the right thing."

Katie huffed. "He lost the race. How can that be *the right thing?* He should have at least tried to win."

Jason frowned at her disapprovingly. "At the risk of injuring King on this hard surface? It looks like King's gate was frozen and it opened a second later than the other gates. You and I both know King probably could have made up the ground and caught the pack, but as hard as this track is, it could have caused him some serious, if not permanent, injury. I know that's not what you want, Kat." He pushed the lead rope and halter into her hands. "Are you willing to risk your horse for a lousy win purse? You're starting to sound like the other trainers."

Katie lowered her eyes. She felt the hot blush of shame race to her cheeks. Jason was right. But it wasn't for herself that she wanted to win so badly—it was for King. She knew how much he loved to challenge the other horses and thunder ahead of the pack across the finish line.

She felt guilty for the bad thoughts she had had about Mark. If she were ever going to be a good jockey, she'd better learn to use good judgment the way he just did. "I'm sorry. I'm being an idiot. Let's go get our horse."

They walked Willow King back to the barn and cooled him out, then loaded him in the trailer and headed for home. It was a quiet ride back to Willow Run Farm.

⊶ *Chapter Six* ⊷

"A gate malfunction," Katie muttered to herself as she dragged the bale of grass hay into the middle of the barn. "Of all the rotten luck!"

Jason had talked to the gate crew last night after he spoke with Mark. They confirmed what the jockey said—because of the frigid temperatures, the starting gate had not tripped all the latches when the button was pressed. Stalls one and ten had misfired. But number ten was unoccupied, so King had the misfortune of being the only horse let out of the gate after all the others. Too late to have a decent go at it. The officials said they would not rerun the race because of one horse's misfortune. The only thing they would do was refund Willow King's jockey fee.

Katie knew in her heart that Mark had done the right thing by reining King in and not allowing him to run. But she wondered if somehow it would have been different if she had been aboard. The thought inspired her to get to work on her jockey's license—with or without Mark.

She pulled the hay hooks from the bale and sat down heavily upon it, catching her breath. The hay weighed almost as much as she did. When her breathing returned to normal, she dragged the second bale over. This was the one that was going to be difficult. She had to stack this bale on top of the other one to make a *hay-horse.*

When she'd first learned to gallop, old John had started her on this no-legged beast. By stacking up two bales of hay and attaching a bridle and saddle, Katie was able to work on the positioning of her reins for regulating a horse's speed and on her balance in the stirrups.

That was the tricky part. The gallop saddle sat on top of the hay-horse, but the girth wasn't attached. As she'd found out countless times, if you leaned a little too far to one side, you fell off.

She winced as she remembered how sore her back and bad leg had been after landing on the packed dirt of the barn floor. She had made several trips to see Dr. Marty during that phase of her training. She hoped her balance was good enough now that she wouldn't have to worry about repeating that scene. After the bad fall she had taken from Willow King's little brother, she didn't know if she could stand another jolt this soon.

"Katie?"

The sound of Mark's voice carried from outside the barn, startling her. What was the jockey doing at her house on a school day, especially this early in the morning? She went to the barn door to meet him.

"Good morning." Mark smiled when he saw her. "Your mother told me you were out here."

Katie gave him a puzzled frown. "What are you doing here?" She had never told Mark where she lived. Somebody at Willow Run must have pointed out her house.

Mark shifted from one foot to the other. "I wanted to talk to you about last night's race. You left before I was done with my last race, and I didn't want to take the chance of missing you at school today." He made eye contact with Katie and smiled uneasily. "It wasn't my fault that the gate malfunctioned last night, and I was kind of hoping that you'd give me another chance. I know I can win on this colt."

Katie crossed her arms and cocked her head, considering the plea. This was the perfect chance to ask Mark to give her jockey lessons. "To tell the truth, I was really disappointed with King's race last night," Katie said. "But I think we can work something out."

"Great!" Mark agreed. "I'll take Willow King to the top! Ever since I first started riding, I promised myself that one day I would ride in the Kentucky Derby. I'm your guy, Katie. I can get the job done." Mark removed his Portland Downs baseball cap and slapped it against his jeans. "Just tell me what I've got to do to seal my end of the deal."

Katie wondered if the wide smile Mark was wearing would suddenly vanish when he heard the bargain. She cleared her throat and pressed home the point. "I'll let you ride Willow King again if you give me lessons on how to be a jockey," she said, hearing the request echo through the empty barn.

To his credit, Mark only faltered a moment, and his smile lost none of its brilliance.

"A jockey," he said, placing his hat back on his head. "That's a mighty tough job for a girl. It's not like galloping, Katie. There's a lot of rough play out there on the race course." He stuffed his hands into his jeans and raised a brow. "Are you sure that's what you want?"

Katie nodded. "I'm a good enough rider," she said with determination. "I just need someone to teach me what it takes to be a jockey."

Mark grinned. "Like I said, I'm your guy."

"So you'll do it?" she said. "You'll teach me?"

Mark nodded his head in agreement.

"Even if it means that I'll eventually be riding Willow King?" Katie watched the emotions play across Mark's face as she waited for that piece of information to sink in. *Maybe even in the Kentucky Derby,* Katie thought.

Mark looked down at the ground, kicking at a piece of dirt, before raising his eyes to meet Katie's. "Sure, why not?" he said, shrugging his shoulders. "It'll be a while before you can get your license, and you might not even like being a jockey."

He tipped his hat to her as he made his way to the barn door. "Besides, I plan to be the best jockey at this race meet. After I win a few races on King, you won't *want* to change riders." He placed a piece of hay between his teeth and gave her a mischievous grin, then exited the barn.

Katie stood there for a moment before realizing just what this bargain meant. She was now on her way to becoming a jockey! "Yes!" she shouted. She quickly stacked the second bale on top of the first and put the saddle and bridle in place. She glanced at her watch. She had a half-hour before she had to catch the school bus. That was enough time to work on using her whip. She didn't want to look like a total beginner when she met Mark for her first lesson.

She climbed aboard the stationary steed and put her feet in the irons, rising into the gallop position to check her balance.

Last year, one of the retired jockeys helping out at Willow Run had shown her how to carry her whip and get it ready for use. She hadn't practiced much because it wasn't necessary to use the crop during the morning workouts. If a horse had to run that fast, its jockey was usually in the irons.

Katie fumbled with the whip, trying to twirl it into the upright, ready position. She dropped it the first three tries and had to get off and pick it up. On the fourth attempt, she was so engrossed in the mechanics that she forgot about balance and felt herself sliding off the side of her straw mount.

Katie hit the ground with a resounding thump, knocking the wind from her lungs. She had taken the saddle with her, and her feet were still tangled in the stirrups. She'd managed to keep hold of the reins, but the whip had flown off the other side.

She lay gasping in the middle of the barn, staring up at the cobwebbed ceiling as the air wheezed back into her body. She thought she heard a chuckle, but at the moment she couldn't turn her head to see if anyone had witnessed her clumsy display. At seven o'clock in the morning, she doubted anyone else was there. It was probably just the little birds she was seeing twittering around her head.

"Geez, Kat, I thought you gave up that *Three Stooges* routine a while ago. And all this time, you've been practicing in private." Jason laughed as he offered her a hand up. "Are you okay? You landed pretty hard."

Katie finally drew a deep breath of air. It burned into her lungs, and she sputtered as she inhaled again. How was it that Jason always managed to catch her in embarrassing situations? She recalled several years ago when King was a baby and she was teaching him to lead. When Jason had entered the barn, Katie was at the end of the colt's lead rope, taking a ride down the aisle on her belly.

She untangled her feet from the stirrups and accepted his hand up. "It's not that funny," she grumbled, dusting the dirt from her backside. What if she fell off in front of Mark? Would he give up on teaching her if he didn't think she could handle it? She might be the owner of Willow King, but the bitter fact was, whether she was owner or not, they would do what was best for the horse. If Mark was the best choice, he would be the one to ride King in the Derby.

"Sorry." Jason tried to wipe the smile from his face, but it wouldn't go away.

Katie felt the hot burn of embarrassment well up in her. *Why can't I be graceful like Cindy? Will I always be such a klutz?* she thought. She jerked the saddle off the dirt floor and plunked it back on top of the hay bales. She bit her lip and counted to ten, turning her back so that Jason wouldn't see how upset she was. All the doubts she had about becoming a jockey came to the surface and refused to be pushed aside.

"What's this?" Jason stepped in front of her and lifted her face for inspection.

She pulled her chin from his grasp and turned her back on him again, angry at herself for letting her emotions get the better of her.

"Katie, what's the matter?" Jason placed his hands gently on her shoulders. "I was only teasing. I would never try to hurt your feelings."

Katie pursed her lips and stared at the old wooden planks of the barn wall. "I know," she whispered, not wanting to look at Jason. "It's...it's just that I try so hard, and sometimes it's not good enough."

Jason sat her down on the hay and offered her an encouraging smile. "What are we talking about here? I remember when John had you riding this old hay-nag to get you *started.* You've been galloping for almost a year now, and you're good at it, so why this sudden urge to ride the fake horse again?"

Katie knew she couldn't hide her secret from Jason anymore. The time had come to tell him of her plan. She snagged a long piece of hay from the top bale and shredded it between her fingers. In a quiet voice she said, "I want to be a jockey."

There was a long pause while Jason considered her revelation.

"Are you sure, Kat? That's a pretty dangerous career," he said.

Katie met his eyes. "I know, but you believe I can do it, don't you?" She felt a heaviness in her heart. Jason had always believed in her. His opinion mattered a lot to Katie.

Jason gave her a lopsided grin and sat down beside her. "Of course you can do it. You can do anything you put your mind to. And you know you can always count on me to help. It's just that...well, I like you a lot, Kat, and I don't want to see you get hurt. You've seen some of the accidents. It happens to the best of them. Even King's first jockey wasn't immune."

Katie's lips trembled as she attempted a smile. She should have known Jason would be on her side. He was just concerned for her.

Jason chucked her under the chin and mussed up her hair. "If you've got your heart set on this, maybe we should talk to someone about giving you jockey lessons."

Katie picked up the whip and placed it on top of the bales. "I've already spoken to someone," she said, not wanting to look Jason in the eye.

"Oh, yeah? Who?" Jason shifted his weight beside her, looking directly into her face.

"I made a bargain with Mark. I've asked him to help me in exchange for giving him some more races on King." Katie hopped off the bale, grabbing the saddle and bridle and carrying them to the tack room.

"I don't know if that's such a good idea," Jason said, frowning. "We can find someone better."

"Better?" Katie raised her eyebrows. "Mark was one of the top riders at Aqueduct in New York. Everyone's saying he's going to be the number-one jockey here this year. Who are you going to get that's better?"

Jason looked a little annoyed. "I guess you're right."

Katie finally faced Jason and gave him a weak smile. "The only thing that really worries me is, what if I'm such a klutz that he gives up on teaching me? He's already got Cindy as a student, and her dad owns one of the biggest racing farms in this area. Why would he bother with someone like me if it wasn't to give him races on King?"

Jason took her hands in his and gave her his best smile. "Like I've told you a gazillion times before, Katie Durham, you're special. He should be thrilled to teach you even without the bargain."

Katie smiled. Jason was the absolute best to think so well of her. Still, she could see there was an anxiousness in his face. Was he worried that she'd fall under the spell of Mark's good looks and winsome smile? She would have to remember who her real friends were and not be blinded by a cute face and exciting career.

Jason looked at his watch. "I came here to give you a lift to school. We better hurry or we'll be late. I'll wait for you in the car."

Katie ran to the house to change her clothes. This was shaping up to be an excellent day!

"Hi there."

The soft New England accent caught Katie totally by surprise. She took one look at Mark's disarming smile and missed the upper shelf of her locker. The math book she was putting away caught the edge of the stack, and all the books tumbled out of her locker, landing in a pile at her feet. The carefully written notes that were stuffed between the pages swirled on the air and floated to the tile a second later, reminding her of a flock of pigeons coming home to roost.

The temperature in the hallway seemed to rise suddenly by ten degrees. Katie slowly exhaled and looked around. The two girls whose lockers were next to hers politely averted their gazes, sparing her more embarrassment. Several popular junior girls hid their snickers behind well-manicured hands. A boy from the football team laughed outright. Katie was mortified.

"Wow! I wish I had that kind of effect on all the girls," Mark said as he stooped to pick up Katie's books.

She knew Mark was joking, but he was closer to the truth than she wanted to admit. She did like him, and because of that, she felt nervous around him. It was going to be difficult taking lessons from Mark if she didn't get over these jitters.

A smart remark from a passing student jolted Katie from her statue-like state. She bent to help Mark pick up her books. Her hands fluttered here and there like butterflies. "I'm really sorry." She avoided looking in his eyes. She didn't want to see him laughing at her too.

"No, I'm the one who should apologize." Mark handed her a stack of books. "I shouldn't have sneaked up on you like that. It's just that I saw you across the hall, and I wanted to catch you before you ran off to your next class."

"Oh?" Katie couldn't think of anything else to say. The single word hung in the air waiting for a few more sentences to join it, but none were forthcoming.

"Yeah. I wanted to talk to you about your lessons," Mark said. "I'm sure you'll want to get started as soon as possible."

Katie smiled as she gathered her widespread notes. "You bet," she said. "I'll be at Willow Run tonight after school if you want to get started."

"That sounds good to me." Mark handed Katie her math book.

The sharp *clack, clack* of heels rang out on the tile, and two ruby-red shoes planted themselves firmly on top of a stray sheet of paper.

"I swear, Katie, you're a walking disaster." Cindy's voice rang out above the ruckus in the hall. "It's a miracle you haven't caused a wreck on the racetrack."

Katie's eyes traveled from the *Wizard of Oz* shoes, over Cindy's fashionable outfit, to the mocking look on her haughty face.

"It was just a little accident," Mark explained. "I was trying to help Katie get something out of her locker, and I dropped all the books." He handed the rest of the papers to Katie and stood to face Cindy.

Katie gave him a quick smile of gratitude. The last thing she needed was to be demeaned by Cindy in the middle of the hall for all to hear and see.

Cindy looped her arm through Mark's and pulled him down the hall, calling back over her shoulder, "Well, that's a first. It's usually Katie who causes the accidents." She gave Katie a tight-lipped smile before turning her attention to Mark.

Mark shrugged his shoulders and waved as he allowed himself to be dragged down the hall. Katie looked at the books that were now neatly stacked in her locker. She felt like knocking them all down and stomping on them, but two spectacles in one day would be a bit much—even for her.

What is it? she asked herself. Did she really like the young jockey? She knew Mark was just out for himself. He was only interested in her because of her horse. But she still felt an attraction to him. Or maybe she was feeling a twinge of jealousy because Cindy always made a point of trying to best her in everything—even boys.

Katie let out a measured breath. Either way, she knew

that she really shouldn't care. She had Jason; and there were things that she would always be good at and things that Cindy would always be good at, like causing discontent among the general population.

Katie laughed to herself. Cindy wasn't worth getting frazzled over. She closed the locker door and set out for her next class. In a few more hours she'd be with Willow King, and she would get to take her first jockey lesson. And that would put her a little closer to riding her first race.

After school, Katie found Camela perched on her bale of straw in King's shed row. The girl lifted her face when Katie walked down the aisle.

"I jumped off the school bus and ran here as fast as I could," Katie told Camela as she opened the tack room door. "How could you beat me? Your school must get out really early."

"I don't go to school," Camela said.

It was a simple statement, but it stopped Katie in her tracks. After an entire week of nothing but a couple of quotes from the kid's grandpa, she hadn't expected Camela to answer. Maybe it was a fluke, and that would be her sentence for the week. Katie resolved to test her.

"What do you mean, you don't go to school? Everybody has to go to school."

"I don't."

"I thought they could throw your parents in jail or something if you didn't go." Katie didn't make a big deal out of Camela's sudden desire to speak. She wanted to know why the girl wasn't in school, but she was afraid if she made a fuss over it, Camela would clam up again. Maybe she could try something that wouldn't take much speaking.

Katie pulled King from his stall and clipped him into the cross-ties, giving the colt a good scratching behind the ears while he nuzzled her pockets for the carrot he knew would be there.

"You're awfully clever," Katie said to King when he found the carrot. She pulled it from her pocket and broke it into several pieces, feeding it to him one at a time. "I need to brush King," she said to Camela. "Would you like to help me brush him?"

Camela vigorously shook her head *no*.

Katie had expected that much. Camela was afraid of horses, but she couldn't remain in a stable and not have any contact with them.

"Just a couple of brush strokes," Katie cajoled. "I'll be right here with you, and I'll guide your hand." But Camela shook her head once again.

Katie shrugged. She had tried. There was nothing else she could do. She bent to pick up a brush, then silently whisked it over King's soft coat, dislodging dust and small bits of hay.

Katie was running the brush over King's hindquarters when he surprised her by taking a step forward, straining at the limit of the cross-ties as he arched his neck toward Camela. Katie let the hand that held the brush drop to her side as she watched Camela sense that King was leaning toward her. *That-a-boy, King,* thought Katie. In very slow motion, Camela began to stretch her palm toward King, inching ever so slowly toward the bay colt's elegant head. King extended his nose. Camela immediately recoiled when her hand came in contact with his whiskers. But the girl decided to venture upward once more, resting her fingers on the soft spot between King's nostrils.

"He's a good boy, isn't he?" Katie said as she went back to grooming King, half surprised by their pleasant interaction.

"I've got a tutor, but what good will it do?" Camela suddenly declared. She spoke again, and her voice turned bitter. "Nobody will let me do anything by myself. Even if they did, what could *I* possibly do?"

Katie was flabbergasted—not only by Camela's sudden declaration of her private thoughts, but also by what they were. Where had Camela gotten such silly notions?

"Camela, just because you're blind doesn't mean you can't live a full life," Katie said. "You just have to make some adjustments."

Camela snorted her disdain. "What would you know about it? You sound just like everyone else with their know-it-all attitudes. You don't know what I go through." She shifted on the hay and gave Katie her back.

Katie sat on the bale next to Camela and bent to untie her shoe. It was the ugly one with the extra-high sole that helped make both her legs the same length when she walked. "You're right, Camela. I don't know what you go through. I can't even imagine what it would be like to be blind. I count my blessings every day that I have my sight."

She put her special shoe in Camela's hands. "But I do know what it's like to have a handicap. Cindy's already told you about my short leg. I know it's not nearly the same as your problem, but believe me, this has caused me more back pain, more mental stress, and more embarrassment than I care to remember."

Camela remained silent. Katie took the hated shoe from the girl and crammed it back on her foot. "Lord knows I've had my own share of pity parties, and there are plenty of things I can't do, but when there's so much I *can do,* why shouldn't I?"

She stood and brushed the straw from the seat of her pants. "You're a smart girl, Camela," Katie said. "There's so much out there to do and learn. Don't waste the opportunity. *My* grandfather used to have a saying: *'Knowledge is power. It's the one thing that nobody can take away from you. You're the one who determines how much you do or don't have.'*"

Katie stood there waiting for a reply, or some kind of acknowledgment that Camela had heard and understood. When none was forthcoming, Katie walked down the shed row. She looked back when she reached the tack room. Camela remained where she was with her back to Katie, but Katie could see the slump in her shoulders and the downcast angle of her face.

Katie jerked open the door. What else could she say? If the kid wanted to wallow in self-pity, Katie could do little to stop her.

She shouldn't care, she told herself. Camela already had a teacher and a family. If they couldn't inspire her, how could she?

Katie's shoes echoed on the wooden floor as she entered the tack room. The empty sound matched the hollow ache she felt in her chest. Like it or not, Camela had gotten under her skin. Why couldn't the girl see that it didn't matter what others thought? She had to learn to go for the things she wanted.

Then it dawned on Katie. There was no difference

between her and Camela. She wanted to become a jockey, but she had been afraid to tell anybody, and she still worried that she wouldn't be good enough. Here she was lecturing Camela, and this whole lesson could have been directed right at her.

Katie sighed as she opened the bandage cabinet and pulled out the two cocoa mugs. In another minute she was heading out the door with two steaming mugs of hot cocoa topped with an extra helping of marshmallows. Chocolate could cure just about anything.

She sat down next to Camela and placed a mug by her hand. "I'm sorry, Cam. I've got no business getting on my soapbox and lecturing you when I'm still scared about training for my jockey's license." She took a sip of her drink and expelled a long breath.

Camela reached for the mug and rolled it between her delicate hands. "I'm sorry I called you a know-it-all. I really don't think that." She plucked out one of the marshmallows and popped it into her mouth.

They drank the chocolate in silence. Katie had a feeling those were the only words she would get from Camela for the rest of the day. But she was wrong. As she gathered the empty cups, wondering what Mark would want to start her on tonight, Camela released another one of her riddles.

"My gramps used to say, *'There's no need to fear the wind if your haystacks are tied down,'*" Camela said.

Katie smiled. She'd have to think awhile to decipher that statement. But at least they were making progress.

⊰ Chapter Seven ⊱

When Mark was finished with Cindy's gallop lesson, he came for Katie.

"Are you ready?" he asked as he strode confidently down the shed row. "I want to begin with some ground work. When you get that down, we'll start working a couple of horses together. How about if we start with the whip? Do you have your stick here?"

Katie grimaced. Using the whip was her weakest point so far. She didn't like using a whip, but some horses needed it to run their best, and most trainers insisted you carry one. Katie nodded, then went to retrieve it from the tack room.

Mark grabbed a bridle and walked to Camela's bale of straw. He straddled it the way he would a horse and pulled his knees up in jockey fashion. "Now, there are two positions for your whip," he explained. "One is with the popper end down, so the whole whip extends toward the horse's front legs, creating as little wind resistance as possible. That's the way you'll want to carry it when you break out of the gate." He showed Katie how to hold it by the handle in the right hand while still gripping the reins.

"The other way is in the upright, ready-to-use position, where the entire whip is above your fist and pointed toward the sky." Mark did a quick flip of the whip, changing from the down to the up position.

"Wow!" Katie said. "That looked really cool. Can you teach me how to do that?"

Mark smiled. "That's what I'm here for." He handed her the whip. "Okay, it's your turn."

Katie took the whip from Mark's outstretched hand and seated herself on the bale of straw. She tried to flip the crop into the correct position, but just as it had done this morning, it flew from her hand and dropped to the ground. She frowned. "It looks a lot easier than it really is," she said.

Mark grinned as he bent down to pick up the whip. "Try it again," he said, handing Katie the whip. "But this time, concentrate on rocking the stick forward a little before you pull it back to swing it into position."

Katie slowed down her movements, concentrating on every detail, but the whip ended up on the ground once again. She crossed her arms and exhaled sharply. At this rate, she wouldn't be ready to ride King in the Derby. The big race was only six weeks away, and she still had *a lot* to learn.

"Don't look so upset," Mark said. "You'll get it. Here, I've got something that'll help." He fished in his pocket and pulled out a rubber band, winding it a couple of times around the whip and once around Katie's middle finger. "This will keep the whip attached to your hand. You can take it off when you get better, but some riders use it all the time. They don't want to take a chance at losing their stick during a race."

"Have you ever lost a whip during a race?" Katie asked.

Mark sat down next to Katie. "Several times," he said with a laugh. "And most of the time it cost me the race."

Katie gave the whip a twirl and was surprised when it did what it was supposed to do. "Have you ever thought about *not* carrying a whip?" Katie asked.

Mark shook his head as he made a small correction in Katie's hand position. "A couple of horses I ride won't run a lick if I'm packing a crop. But I carry one for all my other races. Sometimes you've got to have one."

Mark twirled his whip, snapping it into position. Then he used it on the bale of straw as if it were a horse running down the homestretch. "I was once in a race where it was going to be a dead heat," he said. "Both the horses were crossing the finish line at the same time. An old rider had once told me about tapping your horse under the chin to raise his head." Mark mimicked the winning move in the air.

Katie sat forward, listening intently. "What happened?" she asked.

Mark shrugged his shoulders. "I won by a nose. That's one of those little tricks of the trade you need to learn in order to become a good jockey. Things like that can win you a race. That's why a lot of people like to use experienced riders."

Katie stared at Mark, trying to read his face. Was he trying to tell her that she shouldn't bother trying to ride King in the Derby? "Everyone has to start somewhere," she said.

"You're right," Mark agreed. "A lot of trainers like using

apprentice jockeys so they can get the additional five pounds knocked off the weight assignment." He glanced at his watch. "I've got some homework to crank out. I better get going. But you keep practicing that technique. I'll expect you to have it down by our next lesson."

"Thanks for the help," Katie said. "I'll be here same time tomorrow."

The next week passed in a blur. Katie met with Mark several more times, and she was showing a lot of improvement. It wouldn't be long before they would get to work on breaking out of the starting gate—Katie was really looking forward to that.

Then there were only eight days left before the Jim Beam Stakes at Turfway Park. Everyone was preparing to go to Florence, Kentucky. John had a reserved flight for himself and King. They would leave in a couple of days so King could get there in time to settle in and get used to the track. Mark would meet them the morning of the race. The rest of them would be watching the race from their living rooms.

Katie smiled when she thought of King flying in an airplane. Of course, only John was traveling on a regular flight—King would be in a cargo plane—but it still amazed her that horses could fly.

Katie checked her watch. Mark was due at the barn any minute. They were going to put hard work into Willow King today so that he would travel quietly on the trip. Katie was brushing the big colt when Mark arrived. She finished picking King's hooves, then came out of the stall to speak with Mark.

"I've seen that blond kid before. Who is she?" Mark said, pointing to Camela.

"That's Cindy's cousin Camela. She's staying here for a couple of months."

Mark shook his head. "Poor kid. Imagine not being able to see, hear, or talk."

Katie was about to correct him when she saw Camela raise her finger to her lips in a shushing motion. She didn't want to lie to Mark, but she also didn't want to betray Camela. So she simply nodded her head in agreement with what Mark had said.

"What's she doing out here?" Mark held the stall door for her as she entered with King's tack. "Shouldn't she be in a home or something?"

The thought of Camela locked away upset Katie. *How could Mark say such a thing?* she thought. Katie glanced at him as she put the saddle pad across King's back. He smiled at her without a trace of remorse on his face.

"Good morning, Mark," old John said as he entered the shed row. "Is Katie girl here?"

"In here, John." She fitted the saddle into place and tightened the girth, giving King a mock growl when he turned his head and playfully tugged at his saddle cloth. It was a game he always engaged in when left untied. Katie had learned that the hard way.

She smiled as she remembered a present she had once made for King. When the colt was first broken to saddle, she had made him a beautiful saddle cloth, using the money she earned from cleaning stalls. She spent several days on the project, lovingly cutting and sewing material she thought was fit for a king. However, she soon found out that it took the colt approximately ten minutes of unguarded play to tear the thing to shreds.

"You're a little devil sometimes," Katie said as she tweaked King playfully on the end of the nose. She snapped the tie rope to his halter just as John's face poked over the stall door.

"There's been a slight change of plans," the trainer said as he pulled his hat to a jaunty angle. "King's still going to work today, but he's going to have some company."

Katie stepped from the stall and waited expectantly. They usually worked King alone, but the trainer wanted a fast work, and giving King another horse to work against would do the trick.

"Tom Ellis wants to see Willow's Destiny run today. He's expecting that colt to follow in King's hoofprints."

Katie frowned. Destiny was a year younger than King, and he had just recently been broken. Considering how quickly he had gone to hogging it with her a couple of weeks ago, it was obvious he still wasn't completely schooled. He had been in training for one hundred and twenty days, and he only had a couple of three-eighths breezes under his belt. He had no business working with King.

Katie didn't like questioning John, but she was surprised that he would pick this wayward colt as a working partner for King. "Are you sure this is a good idea?" she said, trying to keep the concern out of her voice.

John pulled the hat from his head and wiped a hand across his face. It was an unconscious gesture that Katie had come to recognize as a nervous twitch. It only served to alarm her more.

"Truth to tell, I don't like the idea one bit," he admitted. "But Tom's pushing really hard on this one. Cindy's birthday's coming up, and it seems he wants to enter the colt on that specific day. He hopes to hand her Destiny's registration papers in the winner's circle."

Katie pursed her lips. She was happy just to get a new halter or leg wraps for King on her birthday. Little Miss Fancy Pants got a whole horse.

John saw her frown. "Don't worry yourself none, girl," he was quick to add. "You don't have to ride Destiny. I've got the kid who broke the colt coming in to do the dirty work."

"Thanks, John, but you know I'd get on him if you wanted me to. I'm not afraid of him."

John turned to Mark. "Why don't you run up to the other barn and catch another horse while we tack up Destiny. We'll be ready in twenty minutes."

Katie heard the muted sound of Mark's riding boots as he jogged down the aisle. The soft patter was quickly followed by a heavy thump. John and Katie turned to see the young jockey sprawled in the dirt just past Camela's bale.

"I'm sorry, Mark. There's a dip in the shed row, and we've been trying to find it. You're the second person to trip on it."

Mark regained his feet and grumbled under his breath. "I'll get that fixed today," Katie promised as he left the barn. She turned to study Camela. The girl sat with her chin tilted toward the rafters, as if studying the birds that roosted there. She seemed oblivious to the events going on around her. But Katie had her suspicions.

"Who do we have here?" John asked as he stopped in front of the young girl.

Katie was surprised that John hadn't met Camela yet, but the trainer had been spending a lot of time at the two-year-old barn lately, leaving the older horses to Jason. "This is Camela," said Katie. "She doesn't talk much."

"Then I guess she's not related to you," John laughed, and slapped his knee.

"Very funny," she grouched, but she joined in his laughter. She could tell by the smile that tugged the corners of Camela's mouth that she liked John's humor too.

"You're welcome in this barn anytime, but we'll have to move you to a better spot," John suggested. "This is right where the horses walk, and sometimes they get a little rambunctious. I don't want you getting hurt."

Katie saw the fearful look that passed over Camela's face. Why would Camela agree to spend her days at the barn when horses seemed to scare her so much? Maybe someday Camela would open up and talk about it. For now, Katie set up a place in the tack room for the young girl to sit.

The clouds were gathering, and there was a chill in the air. While she was moving Camela's chair closer to the heater, she heard Jason's truck pull up. Acting on a hunch, Katie peeked around the corner to watch Jason walk down the apparently difficult shed row.

"Hi, Cam. How's it going?" Jason said as he walked past the danger zone, accepting Katie's smile as his answer. He never once stumbled or took a bad step.

Katie tapped a finger on her chin, puzzling over the situation. Maybe her suspicion was wrong. She shrugged it off and fetched Camela to settle her into the cozy chair.

"How are your lessons with Mark going?" asked Jason. "Will you be ready to ride in the races pretty soon?"

Katie grinned. "I think I'm doing pretty well. Mark says I'm ready to start working horses out of the gate. But I think he's starting to stall me."

"How's that?" Jason said as his brows drew together.

Katie picked up the brush box and moved it out of the center of the aisle. "Mark knows that I want to ride King. He insists that he's still the best choice for King's jockey, but I'm not so sure. King has always worked really well for me. I think Mark's afraid he'll lose his Derby mount if I get my license too soon."

Jason took off his hat and ran a hand through his hair. "Wow, Kat. You told me you wanted to get your jockey's license, but I didn't know you were shooting for the Kentucky Derby."

Katie shrugged her shoulders and bit her lip. She looked deep into Jason's eyes, trying to read if he was happy or doubtful about this new piece of information. "It's something to shoot for," she said noncommittally, but she really wanted Jason's approval.

Jason looked rather stern for several moments. Then a slow smile spread across his face. "I guess if you're going to do it, you might as well shoot for the top."

"That's what I like to hear," Katie said as she gave Jason a hug. "But you've got to keep this quiet for now," she warned. "I don't want a lot of people knowing about this, in case...you know."

Jason put an encouraging hand on Katie's shoulder.

"You're good enough, Kat. Never doubt yourself on that." He gave her a lopsided grin. "I know that once you set your mind to something, you'll do it."

The sound of footsteps echoed in the barn. Jason looked over his shoulder. "Well, speak of Mark and here he is. Were your ears burning? We were just talking about you."

"All good, I hope," Mark joked. "Was Katie telling you about our locker catastrophe?" Mark grinned as he looked from Jason to Katie.

Jason's eyes cut quickly to Katie. "No, I haven't heard about that one yet," he said as a jealous look came over his face. "She'll have to tell me about that one later." He looked pointedly at Katie.

Katie lowered her eyes to the ground. "It was nothing," she mumbled. "I dropped some books out of my locker, and Mark was nice enough to help me pick them up."

She turned from both boys and went to check on King. Was Mark trying to goad Jason? Katie had the feeling that Jason already didn't like the idea of her spending so much time with the young jockey. She hoped the guys wouldn't get in a fight and mess up her jockey lessons. She was getting close to being able to test for her license.

"Our rider's here—let's go," hollered John as he came up the shed row with Destiny's gallop boy.

Suddenly the stable sprang to life. Katie pulled King from his stall and held him while Jason gave Mark a leg up. King gave Katie an affectionate nudge with his nose. Destiny's gallop boy stepped up ready to ride. He was a big kid named Bobby who had wanted to be a jockey but had outgrown the job. Now he rode the tough stock in the barn. He declined help in mounting the horse and swung up easily from the ground. John pulled the pony-horse out of his stall and led the procession up the aisle. Katie handed King to him and got out of the way as Destiny spooked at something and bolted down the shed row.

"Katie, run back and get this colt's blinkers," John ordered. "He's acting a little spooky today. You better grab the ones with the full cup. He doesn't need to be looking anywhere but straight down the track."

When Katie entered the tack room, Camela turned to her, a questioning look upon her face. "It's okay, it's just me," Katie said as she riffled through the head gear, looking for the right set of blinkers. "We've got the horses ready to go. You want to come to the track with us? I can give you a play-by-play of what's happening." She looked expectantly at Camela, but the girl just shook her head and turned away.

"Come on, Katie girl, these colts are ready to go. Let's move!" John called from outside.

She turned to Camela. "I'll be back in a few minutes. I'll tell you how it went." She ran out the door to join the others.

King tossed his head and pranced all the way to the training track. As the wind picked up, it blew through his mane and tail. He bowed his neck, showing off his superb muscle and form. Katie looked on with pride. She envied Mark. He was going to have a great ride on her horse today. She scooted out of the way as Willow's Destiny popped his hindquarters up and shook his head, trying to unseat his gallop boy. Bobby just laughed and reined him in.

John gave last-minute instructions to the riders. "I want a fast work, but keep them under control. This is Destiny's third work. He doesn't need to go as fast as I know King is capable of. Back them up to the finish line so they're warmed up. I want a good six-furlong run."

The riders nodded their heads and backtracked the horses at a trot. Katie took her place on the rail beside Jason. She was so caught up in the moment that she felt it was *she* who was out there on King. She paid special attention to the way Mark handled the colt, hoping to glean some extra bits of knowledge.

Destiny squirreled around, trying to get away from his rider. When that didn't work, he jumped and swung his hindquarters inward, attempting to kick King.

"Watch it, Mark. Easy does it," Katie whispered to herself as she clenched her hands. A low rumble of thunder echoed in the distance. It wouldn't be long before they had a downpour. March was always a wet month in Salem.

The horses turned to face the inner rail, then jogged off in unison. King bowed his neck and loped off on cue, behaving like the class horse he was. King's little brother was on the outside. The younger colt continued to misbehave, changing leads every ten steps and tossing his head wildly, eager for the coming run.

"Care to make a bet?" Cindy asked as she unexpectedly wedged in between Jason and Katie. "I think Destiny is going to be better than King. If Destiny wins, you have to do my stalls for an entire week. If King wins, I'll do your stalls."

Katie should have known Cindy wouldn't have missed this race. Destiny was her favorite horse, which figured, because they acted just alike—bratty and out of control. Katie smiled. "I don't like to wager, but this is one bet I can't pass up. You're on."

How could Cindy possibly think her horse could beat King...unless she had worked something out with Mark? Judging by the sly grin on her face, anything was possible.

A gust of wind blew down the back side of the track, whipping Katie's hair across her face. As she brushed it away, she felt a fat drop of rain pelt her hand. It was quickly followed by another. She leaned on the rail, watching the horses make their way around the bottom turn, heading for the red-and-white–striped six-furlong pole.

King galloped with his ears pricked, waiting for his rider to ask for more speed. Destiny loped sideways, occasionally bumping King with a shoulder or hip.

"Can't you straighten your horse?" Katie heard Mark yell to the other rider, but the rest of the words were lost on the wind as another gust blasted down the stretch.

The rain was a steady drizzle by the time the horses pounded past them, picking up speed as they approached the pole. King's ears were now pinned, and his legs worked like great pistons, digging into the wet sand and throwing a spray of dirt as the horses passed. Willow's Destiny could no longer afford to play at the end of the reins. He dug in and ran beside the big horse, refusing to be left behind.

"Look at them go," Cindy shouted above the clap of thunder that echoed through the valley. "We're going to beat you, Katie Durham. Just wait and see!"

Katie pulled her collar up against the wind, but the rain dripped down the back of her neck. She ignored the discomfort as she concentrated on the two Thoroughbreds that ran neck and neck around the top turn. King edged half a length ahead of Destiny.

"Easy does it. Hold on to him," John coached from atop

the pony-horse at the edge of the track.

As if Mark could hear the instructions, he reined King in, allowing Destiny to catch up to them as they came out of the turn and headed down the homestretch.

"Go, Destiny, go!" Cindy yelled, banging her fist on the rail and jumping up and down.

Katie turned to her with a frown. "This isn't a real race, Cindy. The horses are running on their own. They're not being pushed."

Cindy stuck her tongue out and continued to root for her horse.

Katie knew something was wrong when she saw King's head bobble. "What's happening?" she called to John, who had a better vantage point from the back of his horse.

"Destiny is lugging in, pushing King into the rail," John told her. "Pull him up. Get him out of there, Mark!" he screamed across the field, but there was no way the jockey could hear him.

Katie stood on the rail for a better view. The rain was heavy now, so she could barely see to the front side of the track. The horses were charging down the homestretch, ears pinned. Bobby had Destiny's head turned to the outside, but the colt's big body lugged in, bumping King every four strides. Katie knew they were in serious trouble when John turned his mount and charged off toward the racing colts.

King's head nodded again, and Mark stood in the irons in an attempt to pull him up. King slowed enough to give the rampaging colt a half-length lead.

A loud clap of thunder sounded directly overhead, making Katie jump. At the same moment, Destiny bolted across in front of King's legs. King threw his head into the air, desperately trying to avoid contact, but the colt clipped his front feet. King hit the rail and scrambled for purchase on the rain-slicked track.

Katie froze in place, watching in horror as King stumbled, throwing Mark over his right shoulder. Destiny hit the rail so hard he tumbled over the top of it. Even through the wind and rain, Katie heard Destiny's scream and the panicked cry of his rider as they plowed through the rail, splintering the wood post and railings as they slid to the earth on the other side.

Time hung in the balance as Mark somersaulted over and over through the sloppy mud of the racetrack. Destiny, his saddle hanging on his side, struck out with his front legs, trying to free himself from the debris. Bobby lay amid the wooden litter of what used to be the inside rail. Mark finally rolled to a stop in the middle of the track and lay face-up, as still as a discarded rag doll.

The only sounds Katie could hear now were the heavy patter of rain, the distant roll of thunder, and the jackhammer pounding of her heart.

↔ Chapter Eight ↔

Jason was the first to take action. "Cindy, call an ambulance and the veterinarian!" he hollered as he vaulted over the rail. "Katie, catch King as he comes around and get him back to the barn. You can handle the vet when he gets here."

Katie unlocked her legs from the spot where they were rooted and sprinted across the track as John and Jason ran to the other side. King cantered toward her, his reins dangling free and the stirrups beating against the saddle with each heavy hoof-fall. Her brain felt as if the sluggish mud of the racetrack flowed through it.

As King approached, Katie waved her hands and commanded, "Whoa, whoa." The big horse slowed to a trot and came toward her. She could see the confusion in his eyes. When he was close enough, Katie grabbed for the reins, placing a steadying hand on King's shoulder. She felt the hot stickiness before she saw the red river of blood that flowed over the horse's coat, mingling with the dirt and sweat.

Katie pulled her hand away, staring at the mess that

covered it. *King's blood.* She watched it run down her fingers as the rain washed it away. She snapped out of her shock, quickly checking the severity of her horse's injury.

There was a jagged, four-inch gash where King had been pushed into the inside rail. Katie knew that she had to stop the bleeding–and fast. She pressed her hand over the wound, but King flinched and quickly moved away. The rain continued to pour, washing the blood in streaks down the horse's front leg.

"Easy, easy," Katie pleaded to the panicked racehorse. She knew that she had to get him back to his stall as fast as possible. The wound looked really ugly.

Katie tugged on King's reins to get him under control and start him toward the barn. She glanced over her shoulder at the other side of the track. Jason had a hold on Willow's Destiny and was helping the colt's rider to his feet. John knelt in the mud by Mark's prone form. She strained her eyes to see what was happening, but from her vantage point, it appeared that Mark still hadn't moved.

She quickly said her prayers. *He has to be okay,* she thought. *He was just laughing and talking with everyone at the barn ten minutes ago.* Katie suddenly recalled an accident she'd witnessed at one of the smaller tracks the past summer. *"It's the nature of the business,"* an old jockey had commented. Katie shuddered as a chill raced up her spine.

King took a faltering step, drawing her attention back from the other side of the racetrack. He was still winded and blowing heavily, his nostrils distending to show the pink inner lining. The natural hollow above his eyes was now a deep indentation, indicating how nervous he was.

"Poor baby," Katie whispered as she put a comforting

hand up high on King's neck, where it wouldn't disturb the gaping wound. He lowered his head, plodding steadily toward the barn, but he still jumped nervously at the sound of rolling thunder.

They reached the exit gate and turned right. King's aluminum racing plates clicked against the gravel as they crossed the road that led to the stable.

"Don't worry, ol' buddy, it won't be long now," Katie said as she wiped the back of her hand across her eyes. She knew that now wasn't the right time to cry. King needed her strength. She had to concentrate. "Everything is going to be all right," she said as she walked him steadily toward the barn.

Katie glanced at the wound to reassure herself that she had spoken the truth. Her stomach quickly tightened when she saw the injury. The bleeding hadn't slowed at all. In fact, there was a steady stream now coursing down King's shoulder. Katie looked at the ground and saw the red hoofprint King left each time he took a step.

How many gallons of blood does a horse have? she wondered, frantically. *He can't bleed to death in this short time. He just can't.*

In the distance, Katie heard the muted wail of the ambulance. It was such a forlorn sound. It got louder and louder, until the decibel level in her ears matched the hysterical pounding of her heart.

King snorted and tossed his head in the air, dancing at the end of the reins. He knew his stall was near, and he wanted to be in it. Katie tried to hold him back, but it was no use. The rim of white that showed when King rolled his eyes told her that he was beyond his usual common sense.

She trotted with him to the barn, yelling at Camela as

they jogged up the shed row. The girl's face poked out of the tack room. "There's been an accident, Cam. The ambulance is here for the two riders. Willow King's been hurt. I've got to meet the vet." She handed the reins to Camela. "I need you to hold him while I get this saddle off."

Katie heard the sharp intake of breath at the same time King's reins hit the wooden floor.

"I can't," said Camela. The words were almost a sob as the girl backed violently away, tipping over buckets and scattering saddle pads as she went.

King tossed his head and pawed the ground. Katie reached for him before he took off down the shed row. Then she looked at Camela. The girl was plastered against the tack room wall, her arms outspread across the bridles and martingales that hung there. Her vacant eyes now held the same terrified look that King's did.

"What in the world...?" Katie pulled on King's reins and placed a calming hand on his neck, coaxing him to be still enough so that she could see what was wrong with Camela. "What's the matter, Cam?"

The ambulance siren now blared down the back side of the barn. King blew a warning snort and tried to break free. His hooves began echoing loudly as they beat a rapid tattoo on the packed dirt of the barn aisle.

"Get him away from me! Don't let him hurt me!" Camela screeched as she slipped down the wall, curling into a tight ball on the floor.

The feeling of chaos quickly began to spread to the other horses in the barn. Their distress calls bounced off the roof and were picked up by horses in the neighboring stable. Cousin Millie kicked the sides of her stall, while others pawed at doors and neighed their panic.

Camela's terrified whimpers pierced Katie's confounded mind. This was no game. Camela was genuinely petrified with fear. Katie had to do something quick before the medics had to make room for Camela in their rescue vehicle.

Moving as fast as she could, Katie put King in his stall and removed his bridle and saddle. Then she ran back to the tack room. Camela was still on the floor, but she was sitting up with her back against the wall, hugging her knees and trying to quiet her sniffles while she rocked herself back and forth.

Katie sat down beside her and placed a reassuring hand on her arm. "I'm here, Cam. You're okay," she said.

Camela wiped her eyes on the sleeve of her sweatshirt. "I...I know," she sputtered between gulps of air.

"What just happened?"

"Nothing."

"Camela, you were hysterical. Don't tell me that *nothing* just happened."

Camela drew a steadying breath, hiccuping several times before she was able to speak. "I'm afraid of horses, okay? I'm *really* afraid of horses. I thought King was going to trample me."

A disbelieving *tsk* escaped Katie's lips. "I know you're a little nervous around horses, but how could you be at the barn almost every day if you were *this* afraid?"

"Sometimes I'm not afraid," Camela said. "Besides, I wasn't that close to them. When you were moving the horses around, I was always in the feed room or here in the tack room."

"So I guess my next question is, why are you afraid of horses?" asked Katie.

"I don't want to talk about it," Camela quickly snapped. "You said King was injured. You better get the vet."

Katie rocked back on her heels. "Are you going to be okay if I leave you?"

"Of course. I'm not a baby. Hurry up and go fix your horse," said Camela as she crossed her arms and pressed her lips closed.

It appeared that Camela was back to her usual stubborn self. Katie figured that this meant she would probably be okay. Katie knew that Camela was avoiding her question, but she didn't have time to pry the answer out of her right now. She needed to get to the house to make sure the vet was on the way. And Katie didn't trust Cindy to get the information right.

"I'll be back in a minute. This conversation isn't finished," she warned Camela as she exited the tack room.

Katie ran down the aisle as fast as her legs would carry her. The rain was still pounding when she started up the hill to the house. The ambulance drove past as she reached the front porch. She could see Bobby sitting up talking to a medic, but Mark was laid out on the stretcher with an oxygen mask covering his face. She said another quick prayer that he would be all right, then banged on the door of Tom Ellis's house.

Cindy answered the door. She looked pale and in shock.

"Did you call the vet?" Katie said, brushing her wet hair off her forehead.

"Yes, he should be here any minute. Come in," Cindy said, stepping aside so Katie could enter. "I saw the ambulance just went past. It…it…didn't look like Mark was moving." She wrung her hands as she sat on the couch, pulling her feet up under her.

"I've never had anyone get seriously hurt on one of my horses before," Cindy said.

She looked so miserable that Katie felt sorry for her. Sometimes it was easy to forget that the girl actually had a heart. Katie reached out and squeezed Cindy's hand. "He'll be okay. He was wearing his hard hat. And from where I stood, I don't think any of the horses stepped on him. He was probably knocked out when he hit the ground. It was my horse he got hurt on. Believe me, I'm not feeling so hot about it either."

"But it was my horse that caused the accident," Cindy admitted.

Cindy lowered her head and looked as if she was ready to cry. Katie felt really awkward. What could she say? Everything Cindy said was true. Her horse had caused the accident, but she wasn't to blame.

Katie sat there with Cindy. They had never been close friends, yet because they were facing this trouble together, Katie felt they were kindred spirits at this moment. "It's not your fault, Cindy. Horses are big animals, running at a very fast speed. It doesn't take much for an accident to happen. Destiny wasn't ready for that work. But you weren't the one who ordered it."

At that moment, Tom Ellis entered the room. Both girls looked at him, then back at each other. Katie could tell by the look that passed between her and Cindy that they both understood that even responsible adults could make big mistakes.

"Grab your coat, honey. We're going to the hospital to check on the boys. Do you want to come along, Katie?" asked Mr. Ellis.

"Thanks, but I've got to wait for the vet. King's got a pretty nasty cut on his shoulder."

Mr. Ellis frowned. Katie could tell he regretted his rash decision to work Destiny with the stable's prize horse. But it was too late to change anything. All they could do now was pick up the pieces and hope everything turned out okay. Cindy and her father shrugged into their coats and headed for the door.

"Oh, there is one thing," Katie said, stopping their departure. "Camela was really terrified at the barn just now. She said she was afraid of horses and that she thought King was going to trample her. What's that all about?"

Cindy and Tom Ellis stared at each other, seeming to make a silent decision about a family matter. Tom closed the door and cleared his throat.

"Camela hasn't always been blind," he said as he swept the hat from his head and sat down heavily on the chair by the door. "She lost her sight in a riding accident a year ago."

Katie breathed a heavy sigh. No wonder the kid had acted the way she did.

"Her mother sent her here to stay with us for a while," Mr. Ellis continued. "We're all hoping that if she faces her fear, she might be able to conquer it and get better."

Cindy stepped forward. "That's why I've been bringing her down to the barn to sit with you. I know you think I'm being really selfish, and I admit that Camela drives me crazy, but she's the one who asked to sit near the horses. But maybe it's too much for her."

The veterinarian's truck pulled into the driveway. "I have to go," Katie said as she zipped her coat and pulled up her collar. "Thanks for the information. It clears up a lot of things."

Tom Ellis put a large, fatherly hand on her shoulder. "We'd appreciate anything you could do to help. Otherwise, maybe she's better off staying clear of the barn."

"No, I don't think she should," Katie said. "I like Camela. She's kind of grown on me. Don't worry, I'll look after her."

Katie opened the door and hailed Dr. Marvin. He stopped the truck, and she jumped in. They didn't have a lot of daylight left. But even if it was dreary because of the rain clouds, it was still better than stitching a horse by lightbulb after the sun went down.

King was in the aisle getting a bath when they pulled up to the barn. Jason was holding him, and John was doing his best to clean the wound without causing King too much discomfort.

"Let's see what we've got here." Dr. Marvin set his medical bag down on a bale of hay and stepped to King's side. After several *umm*s and *uh-uh*s and a little poking that had King dancing on the end of his lead shank, he proclaimed the wound a nasty laceration and gave the colt a sedative in preparation for stitches.

King's head drooped as the tranquilizer took effect. By the time the vet was done cleaning the wound and was ready to stitch it, King's head was almost touching the ground.

"Katie, hand me that twitch and let's get to work."

Katie steadied her horse while the doctor made skillful

sutures, pulling the ends of the jagged flesh together. When he was finished, he stepped back to regard his handiwork.

"He'll have a scar, but as long as those stitches hold, it'll be a small one. I'm going to leave you some Bute paste to give him before you go to bed tonight and when you get up tomorrow. I want you to keep him pretty quiet for the next twenty-four hours. Then you can hand-walk him a couple times each day."

"How long before it will heal?" Katie asked as she felt the burn of tears sting the backs of her eyes again. She knew that her horse was in a lot of pain, and it killed her to think there was nothing she could do about it.

"It'll be at least ten days before the stitches can come out," Doctor Marvin said. "But don't look so upset. He's actually pretty lucky. His injuries could have been much worse."

Katie thought of the Jim Beam Stakes. It was only eight days away. Several of King's rivals for the Kentucky Derby were entered. Nobody believed that a little-known horse from a small Oregon farm could run with the best colts in the country. The Jim Beam was supposed to be a proving ground for King.

The vet washed his hands in a bucket of soapy water and dried them on a clean towel. "What I can't believe is that Willow's Destiny took out an entire section of rail and turned it into kindling, then managed to come out of it with only a few minor scratches. From the way Cindy described the accident, that horse is lucky he doesn't have a broken leg."

Katie looked at Willow's Destiny. He stood at the front of his stall, pawing the door and calling for his dinner. Katie felt it wasn't fair that he had caused the accident but it was King who stood there filled with tranquilizers to dull his pain.

"Let's hope your riders fared as well as that colt did." The vet patted King on the haunches and held the stall door while Katie led the horse in and removed his halter.

She nodded her head in agreement. It was bad enough that her horse was injured—the boys just *had* to be okay.

~ *Chapter Nine* ~

When the phone in the tack room rang a few hours later, Katie quickly jumped up and answered it.

"Hello?"

"Katie, this is Cindy. We just got back from the hospital. I thought you'd want to know how the guys are doing."

"Are they okay?" Katie took a deep breath and prepared herself for the news.

"Believe it or not, there's no broken bones. Bobby was pretty banged up, but he didn't even need stitches. Mark was worse off, but he's going to be okay."

Katie expelled the breath she had been holding, blowing the hair off her forehead. "Wow. After seeing him go down and just lie there the whole time, I was almost afraid he was..."

"Me too," Cindy agreed. "I never said anything because I didn't want to jinx him. He landed on his head and it knocked him out. He's got a concussion, and the doctors want to hold him overnight to make sure he's all right, but he can come home tomorrow."

"Whew, that's great news." Katie remained silent for a

moment, thinking about how lucky they all were. She could sense that Cindy was doing the same. "Thanks for calling, Cindy. I'll see you at school tomorrow."

Katie hung up the phone and rocked back in her chair, thinking of everything that had happened that day. It was amazing how fast things could change in the racing world. King was entered to run in the richest Derby prep race. Now he couldn't. Mark was supposed to ride at Portland Downs this weekend. Now it was doubtful that the doctor would let him. And how did she feel about riding, now that she had seen some of the dangers up close? The thought of going down in a wreck like that chilled her to the bone. But the one thing her bum leg had taught her was that you couldn't *not* do something because of the *what-if*s. She'd just have to be as careful as she could and hope that God was looking out for her.

Her wandering mind turned to Camela. By the time the vet had arrived and they'd met Jason and John at the barn, the kid was gone. No one had seen her. Perhaps one of the grooms had taken her up to the house?

She didn't know what she would do with Camela, but one thing was for sure—she had to help her get over her fear of horses. The girl would be a danger to herself and others if she had such a violent reaction every time a horse got close to her.

Katie stretched and rubbed her eyes. She would have marched up to the house right now and brought Camela to the barn, but so much had happened. She was bone tired—definitely too tired to fight with a stubborn young girl.

Katie decided to go home and pour her heart out to her mother while they sat on the couch and drank hot cocoa.

She knew that would make her feel better. She also figured to get a good night's sleep so she'd be prepared to do battle with Camela in the morning. And there was no doubt about it in Katie's mind—Camela *would* put up a fight.

Mark wasn't at school the next day, but Katie hadn't expected to see him. When she returned to the farm in the afternoon, she didn't think she'd run into him at the stable either. She walked carefully down the aisle of King's barn, stopping to see how he was doing. King nickered and came to the door when she poked her head into his stall.

"How are you doing, ol' boy?" Katie let herself into the stall and inspected the wound. King's muscles twitched when she examined the stitches. The wound still looked nasty, but she could tell it was healing.

She hugged King before leaving. King returned the affection with a gentle rub of his nose on Katie's chin. It was as if the colt was telling his owner not to worry, that he would be okay.

Katie noticed that Camela's bale of hay sat empty at the end of the shed row. It was something Katie had expected to see. She decided that as soon as she gave King his dose of painkillers, she would go to the house to get Camela.

As she got King's Bute from the medicine cabinet, Katie listened to the sounds of the barn. It was race night at Portland Downs, and all the farm's entries for the night, along with their grooms, had left for the racetrack early that morning. The place was practically deserted now.

Katie gave King his medicine, laughing when the big colt turned up his lip at the bitter taste. She ran a hand over his forelock. "You're a big horse. Take it like the Derby winner you're going to be." She closed his door and put away the medicine, then walked the path to the big house on the hill.

Katie paused a second before she knocked. What if Camela really didn't want to return to the barn? She couldn't very well throw her over her shoulder and *make* her go. She rapped several times on the wooden door. One way or another, she'd convince Camela to return to the barn with her.

Mrs. Ellis opened the door.

"Is Camela here?" Katie shifted from one foot to the other, trying to peer into the living room to find Camela.

Mrs. Ellis opened the door wider to let Katie pass. "She's in her room, at the end of the hall."

Katie nodded her thanks and proceeded down the hall. "Camela?" she said as she tapped on the bedroom door. It opened a few inches, and Katie could see the young girl sitting on her bed.

"What do you want?" Camela said in a sullen voice as she flipped one long braid over her shoulder and put on a haughty face that reminded Katie very much of Cindy.

"I wanted to know if you would like to go to the barn today," replied Katie.

Camela shook her head furiously. "No."

Katie moved into the room and sat on the edge of the lacy bedspread. "King misses you. He didn't see you on your straw bale tonight." She tried to put a smile into her words, but she wasn't sure if it was working.

Camela sat with her back to Katie, acting as if she hadn't heard a word.

Katie sighed. "Look, Cam. I know you can hear me.

Let's not play this game. And…to tell you the truth…I know about your horse accident too." Camela's spine stiffened.

"How do you know about that?" she demanded.

Katie plucked at the hem of the bedspread. "I wasn't snooping," she said. "After what happened yesterday in the barn, I knew your reaction wasn't a regular fear like non-horse people get. So Mr. Ellis told me what happened."

"So?" Camela said stubbornly.

Katie rubbed the back of her neck. She was at a loss for words. How could she convince Camela to return to the barn with her? Then she spotted a couple of horse statues and several photos of Camela on a horse. Camela must have brought them with her from home. It was obvious that she still *liked* horses, despite her fear.

So Katie tried another tack. "When I was little and my folks were first teaching me to ride, I fell off of this pony at a stable, and I didn't want to get back on," Katie said, noting that Camela was beginning to show some interest. "My father told me I had to get right back on or I'd probably always be afraid to ride. I was so scared, but I knew I wanted to be around horses, so I gathered my courage and got back on."

Silence hung in the air. Then Camela spoke. "But I don't want to ride. How can I when I'm blind?"

Katie reached out and took the hand that rested in Camela's lap. The girl snatched it right back.

"Look, Cam," Katie said. "Nobody's expecting you to get right on a horse, but I've got this feeling that you still want horses in your life. And there's no way for that to happen unless you come back to the barn and work on overcoming your fear."

Katie could feel the slight change in Camela's attitude. "The longer you wait, the more difficult it's going to be," she prodded.

Camela heaved a resigned sigh and turned to face Katie. "I *do* want to work with horses again," she stated emphatically. "But I can't help myself. I get really scared."

"It's not going to be easy to get over that," Katie said. "You've got to take it one step at a time. And the first step is to get back to the barn."

Camela leaned down and felt across the floor, locating her shoes. "Let's get to the barn quick before I change my mind," she said suddenly.

Katie led Camela back to the stable. She could feel the girl's hand shaking when they entered King's shed row and the horses poked their heads over the stalls and nickered. "It's okay, Cam," Katie assured her. "They're all in their stalls."

The girls reached the end of the shed row, and Camela took her place on the bale of straw. She folded her delicate hands in her lap and stared out into space with a dejected look on her face.

"Are you all right?" asked Katie.

Camela shrugged her shoulders. "I guess. I'm just not sure how you're going to help me. What do I have to do?"

Katie snapped the lead shank on the old pony-horse. She would have preferred to use King, but she didn't want to take any chances that he might remember Camela's shrieking and act up. It wouldn't do Camela, or King's shoulder, any good.

"I'm bringing a horse out to put in the cross-ties," Katie warned, noting that Camela immediately began to fidget.

"It's just the old pony-horse. He's as gentle as they come."

"What do you want me to do?" Camela asked with a quiver in her voice.

Katie went to Camela and took her hand. "I can't think of any other way than to just jump right in," Katie said as she walked the young girl toward the gray Appaloosa that stood in the cross-ties. "I know you're going to be scared, Cam, but that's okay. I'm going to be right here to make sure that nothing happens to you."

Katie stopped in front of the old horse. "This is Appy. Why don't you pet him and let him sniff you before we brush him."

Camela slowly raised her hand, feeling the air for the horse's head. Appy met her hand halfway and blew gently on her fingers. Camela flinched, but she forced her hand to stroke the horse's soft muzzle. Her look of concern was momentarily replaced by a slight smile. She raised her other hand to cup the pony-horse's nose, and a veil of sadness passed over her features.

"What's wrong?" Katie asked.

Camela shook her head, and a tear slipped down her cheek. "My horse used to tickle me with his whiskers. He had really long whiskers, just like this one."

Katie picked up the brush box and sat it next to Appy. "What happened to your horse?"

Camela frowned. "My parents couldn't stand looking at him after the accident, so they sold him."

"I'm sorry," Katie said as she took Camela's hand and guided her to the side of the horse.

"It didn't matter anyway," Camela said as she accepted the brush that Katie put in her hand. "I couldn't have ridden him again anyway."

"Nonsense," Katie said. "With your stubborness, I believe you can do anything you put your mind to. And right now, I want you to put your mind to brushing this old horse." She placed the soft brush in Camela's trembling hand and gently lifted it to the horse's neck, stroking in a downward motion. After a couple of passes, she let Camela do it on her own.

After a moment, the pony-horse breathed a contented sigh and relaxed.

"I recognize that sound," Camela said as she began to relax too.

Katie stayed close, guiding the girl around the horse's hindquarters so that she could brush the other side. Everything was going well until Appy blew through his lips. It completely startled Camela.

"What happened?" Camela cried as she jumped back, bumping into the barn wall and scraping her elbow.

"It's okay," Katie assured her as she grabbed Camela's arm and escorted her back to her seat. "Appy just had a tickle in his nose and was trying to get rid of it. Hey, that was pretty good for your first brush job," she added.

Camela brightened a bit. "You think so?"

"Sure," said Katie as she put the brush box away and unsnapped Appy to lead him back to his stall. "That's the longest I've ever seen you stand next to a horse. You brushed almost all of him. I'd say that's really good."

Camela smiled for a moment, then lowered her head as a frown overcame her. "Yeah, but it's still not much of an accomplishment," she said.

Katie took a seat next to Camela on the bale. "What do

you mean? I think you've made a huge leap."

Camela flared up again. "So I brushed a horse. What good is that? I'm still useless!" she exclaimed, turning away from Katie.

Katie placed a gentle hand on her new friend's shoulder. "What's this all about, Cam? I thought you were happy about being near a horse."

Camela sniffed a couple of times. "Nobody wants me. I...I'm useless. I'm blind, and I...I...can't do anything, so nobody wants me anymore," she stammered.

For a moment, Katie just stood there, not knowing what to do or say. "Hush now, everything's going to be okay," she said finally, as she remembered the things her mother did to comfort her when she was feeling down. She stroked Camela's hair and rubbed the place between her shoulder blades.

"That's not true," answered Camela. "What makes you think that?"

Camela drew her knees to her chest and propped up her chin. She dragged her sleeve across her face and sniffed. "My mother sent me here to get me out of her hair. Uncle Tom told Cousin Cindy that it was her responsibility to keep me entertained, and she pawned me off on you. I'm afraid that if no one wants me anymore, they'll send me away for good."

"Why would they do that?" Katie said, handing her a crumpled tissue she found in her pocket.

"Because I'm no good for anything anymore." Camela sniffed again.

"You know that's not true," Katie said, placing her arm around the kid's slight shoulders. "Your mother sent you here hoping you'd face your fears and get out of the funk you've been in. I'm sure your uncle turned you over to Cindy because he thought you'd have more fun with someone your own age. And Cindy...well, we both know how selfish she can be, but she thought you would have more fun being here with me."

Camela lifted her face. "I want to get better. I want people to like me. But how can they when I'm just this lump of clay and I can't do anything?"

Katie heaved a sigh. "If that's how you feel about yourself, then that's how you're going to be." Katie shook her head in disbelief. "Camela, about the only thing I wouldn't trust you to do right now is drive a car."

A smile came to Camela's face. Katie felt a ray of hope and pressed on.

"Taking the first step is always frightening, but it's the only way you'll be able to do those things you used to like," Katie said.

"Do you really think I can be normal again?" Camela dried the last of her tears on the tissue.

Katie laughed. "What's *normal?* Everyone thinks Cindy is normal. But do you want to be like that?" Camela shook her head violently. "Phooey on normal–let's shoot for spectacular!" said Katie.

Camela chuckled and then turned to face Katie with a serious look on her face. "I can't do this by myself. Sometimes I get so scared that I just want to quit. Promise me you'll help and not let me give up, even if I want to."

"Of course I will. But you've got to let me help you," Katie said. "You've got to push past this fear of yours, no matter how much it scares you."

"I'll try," Camela said.

Katie took Camela's arm and helped her up. "You did really well today. Now it's time to get you back to the house. I've got to finish up a few small chores and get home before my dinner gets cold."

When Katie dropped Camela off at the front door, the girl looked back over her shoulder and waved. "I'll see you tomorrow morning, Katie. I won't let you down."

"I know you won't, Camela." Katie returned the wave and headed back to the barn. She couldn't help but hope that *she* wouldn't let *Cam* down.

⤙ Chapter Ten ⤚

Katie woke when the first rays of dawn poked through the curtains and spilled across her pillow. She rolled to the edge of the bed and peeked outside. The sky was so bright that she had to squint against the sun's early-morning glare. She scrambled out of bed and pulled on her jeans. It was rare to get such a fine day in the middle of March. She didn't want to waste a minute of it.

Katie padded down the hallway to the kitchen, where she had breakfast with her mother. They talked about King's upcoming races, as well as the progress Katie had made with her jockey lessons. Although Mark hadn't been to the stable in several days, it hadn't stopped Katie from practicing her riding form. She placed her empty cereal bowl in the sink and kissed her mother good-bye before bolting out the door to Willow Run Farm.

The horses nickered a greeting when Katie entered the stable. They all bobbed their heads and pawed at their doors, anxious for breakfast.

"Okay, okay, your oats are coming." She stopped beside Willow King and gave him a quick scratch behind the ears before entering his stall. "How's the war wound, ol' buddy?" She winced when she saw the sutured cut. She reached out to remove a piece of hay that had stuck to the drying blood, but King shied away, twitching the muscles in his shoulder as if he were shooing away a fly.

"Easy, boy," she crooned. "I'm not going to bother it now, but we'll have to clean it up later." She gave King another affectionate scratch and then ducked out of the stall to serve up the morning feed.

As Katie moved from stall to stall dumping a measure of oats into each bucket, she thought about what she could do to help Camela overcome her fears. Camela had made some progress yesterday, but Katie wasn't content. She wanted more. And she knew Camela wanted more too.

When she finished with the oats, she returned the empty buckets to the feed shed. Her eyes suddenly lit upon a coil of rope that was stashed in the corner under a pile of empty grain sacks. Her mind began racing with possibilities. She pushed aside the dusty sacks, dragged the rope outside, and carefully unwound it. It was in one piece and extra long. Then the idea came to her—and she smiled. She knew exactly what to do.

The sound of a truck engine and the slam of a vehicle door alerted Katie that Cam was on the way. When she heard the *tock, tock, tap* of Camela's cane echoing down the shed row, she poked her head out and smiled. "Good morning, Cam. You ready to get started?"

Camela stopped outside the stall Katie was cleaning. "Sure, might as well get to it." Camela put on a brave smile, but Katie could hear the tremble in her voice and see the knuckles of her fingers turn white as she gripped her cane.

"I've only got a half-hour before Cindy comes to get me," Camela explained. "I'm going to the races with them today. I don't know why they bother—I can't see anything. I'd much rather stay here."

Katie threw the last of the dirty straw into the wheelbarrow and set the pitchfork outside the stall. "I wish I could trade places with you. I *love* going to the races. Even if you can't see what's happening, the announcer keeps a running tally of where each horse is during the race. There's people cheering and so much hustle and bustle everywhere that..." She paused and then shrugged her shoulders. "I don't know how to describe it. It's just something that you've got to experience for yourself. I think you'll like it."

"Shall I talk to my uncle to see if you can come with us?"

"Thanks, Cam, but I've got to stay here and watch over things. Most of the other grooms are at the racetrack with your uncle's stock. Someone's got to feed, and it's my turn this week."

"Oh," Camela said, with disappointment in her tone.

"Go and have a good time," Katie encouraged her. "There will be horses everywhere—it'll be like an adventure. Think of it as part of your training. And speaking of training...how about helping me out this morning? I need to doctor King's shoulder and take him for a short walk to help get the stiffness out. So could you get the afternoon feed ready for me while I take care of my horse?"

Camela gave a sarcastic snort and propped her fist on her hip. "Sure, I'll just march right down there and gather all the stuff and put it exactly where you want it."

"I know you will," Katie said with confidence.

Camela laughed outright. "I'm beginning to think Mark wasn't the only one that fell on his head. Are you *crazy?* I can't see, *remember?* How am I supposed to do all that when I don't know where anything is?"

"Come here and let me show you." Katie wanted to chuckle when she saw the disbelieving look on Camela's face, but she restrained herself for fear that Cam might think she was making fun of her. "Take hold of my arm, and let's start at the end of the shed row."

Since the stable was laid out as a long row of stalls with the roof extending over the aisle, there were lots of support poles to help Katie with her plan. She took Camela's hand and placed it on the rope that she had tied to each pole. "Feel this?"

Camela nodded her head, but a frown creased her brow. "It feels like a rope to me. How's this supposed to help anything?"

"Ahhh, now that's the fun part." Katie grabbed the girl by the elbow. "Keep your hand on the rope and follow me." They walked several steps before Camela's fingers found the first large knot in the line.

"What's this?" The girl plucked at the lump.

"That's your first stall in the barn."

Camela still had a puzzled look on her face, so Katie moved her forward again, stopping at the second knot in the rope. "Feel that knot? This is the next stall," Katie said, and she smiled in triumph when she saw the light of understanding dawn on Camela's face.

This time Camela moved forward on her own, finding the next three knots and their corresponding stalls. Then she continued on. When she reached two side-by-side lumps in the rope, she paused. "What does it mean when there are two of them?" She worked her fingers over the knots again and again, trying to fathom their meaning.

Katie patted her on the back. "That means you've reached the tack room."

Camela turned back the way she had come. "Then Willow King must be knot number five, because he has the stall right before the tack room."

"That's right!" Katie applauded the girl's success, then laughed as Camela did a little jig and clapped her hands.

"What's next?" Camela felt down the rope, finding the next several stalls, the marker for the hose, the gap in the rope for the hotwalker exit, and finally the feed shed.

Katie stopped beside her. "Just remember that the whole front of the shed is open, and there's a step up to get into the feed room." She took Camela by the hand and walked her into the enclosure. "Hay is always on the left, and the grain and feed buckets are always on the right. Any tool you need to open the hay or an oat sack will be on a barrel in the middle between the two. You got that?"

Katie was surprised when Camela turned and flung her arms around her neck.

"I can't believe you did this for me. I promise to try my hardest." The girl dropped her arms and quickly stepped back, as if embarrassed by her sentimental display.

Katie hugged her back, not caring that she squirmed in protest. "That's what friends are for, Cam. Now, *friend,* could you set up my lunch menu so I can take care of King?"

At Camela's eager nod, Katie gave her instructions to set out one can of oats and one flake of hay for each horse.

Then Katie grabbed King's halter and lead rope and pulled him out of his stall.

She paused at the end of the barn, watching Camela work. At first all she could hear was a happily whistled tune and the sound of ten metal feed cans banging around in the shed. But it wasn't long before the girl emerged with her arms loaded with feed and worked her way down the rope to each knot, placing a single can of grain beside each stall door.

Katie didn't want Camela to know she was spying on her, so she turned King and walked off before the girl reached the end of the barn.

King's hooves clicked on the gravel as they crossed the drive that circled the stable area. When they reached the dirt path, Katie patted King high on the neck, and he dropped his elegant head lower to accommodate her.

"I think this is going to work out fine," she told the horse as they plodded together down the path. "Camela already seems to have more confidence. Now, if we can just get you patched up and keep you sound for the Kentucky Derby, everything will be great."

King eyed the long stems of green grass growing along the side of the path and tugged Katie toward them, stretching his lips in an attempt to grab a mouthful before she could stop him.

"Oh no you don't." Katie pulled hard on the lead rope. "This is where the other grooms take the sick horses to graze when they can't work out. You're in bad enough shape already; we don't need you getting sick on top of that. Let's get back to the barn and get this cut cleaned up." She led the big bay horse back to his stall, admiring the elegant sweep of his stride, even with the hurt shoulder.

Camela was sitting on her straw bale when they returned. She beamed like a flashbulb at a photo finish. There was a grain can and a flake of hay in front of each stall.

"You did it," Katie exclaimed. "You really did it!"

Camela broke into a toothy grin and nodded. "It wasn't that hard once I got the hang of the rope."

"That is so cool," Katie said, and laughed when King bobbed his head in apparent agreement. "Look, Cam, even King thinks so." She started to move King forward but quickly stopped when she remembered Cam's fear. "I've got to get King past you so I can put him in his stall."

"No problem." Camela felt for the rope, then hopped off the bale and stood on the other side of it.

Katie moved King down the aisle and put him in his stall. Camela was back on her perch by the time Katie closed the door and turned around. "I'm really proud of you, Cam. What do you say we celebrate your success with a mug of cocoa?"

"Sounds good to me, but you better hurry—Cindy will be here any minute now."

Katie bustled around the tack room. Just when she was pouring the hot water, she heard Cindy's noisy entrance. The girl must have been wearing her new boots, because the *clop, clop, clop* was as loud as a horse's hooves.

"Katie, are you here?" Cindy hollered.

Katie peeked around the corner in time to see Cindy march past the sitting Camela. Just as Cindy drew parallel with her cousin, Camela's cane snaked out with lightning speed and tangled in her feet. Cindy hit the ground with a resounding thump, and Camela flashed a triumphant grin before turning serious.

"Are you okay, Cousin Cindy?"

Cindy picked herself off the packed dirt, examining her skinned palms. "Katie Durham, I told you to fix this shed row. Now look what's happened!"

Katie examined Cindy's abrasions. "I've got some Band-Aids in the medicine cabinet. Let me get you one."

Cindy snatched her hand away, giving Katie a withering glare. "I'll do it myself," she said as she stomped down the aisle, disappearing into the tack room.

Katie approached Camela, bending down to her ear level and speaking in a hushed tone. "I can't believe you just did that."

"Did what?" Camela feigned innocence.

"You know exactly what I mean. I saw you trip your cousin." A thought occurred to her. "Then you must have been tripping her all along—and Mark too!"

Camela folded her hands in her lap. "Well, they deserved it. They're both mean."

Katie glanced up to make sure Cindy was still in the tack room. Then she turned her gaze back on Camela. "So what does that make *you* for doing it?"

"Happy?" Camela answered.

Katie shook her head. "Camela, you're unbelievable!"

As Cindy left the tack room, she grabbed her cousin by the arm. "Let's get out of here, Camela. I've got to change my clothes before I can go to the races." Cindy looked back and pointed an accusing finger at the scene of the accident. "I want that fixed by tomorrow, Katie, or I'm telling my father."

Katie smiled sweetly. "It's already been fixed. Cam and I took care of it while you were bandaging your hand. *Didn't we, Camela?*"

The girl nodded her head in agreement. "That's right. Katie and I got rid of that snag while you were busy. I don't think you'll have a problem with it anymore."

"I certainly hope not." Cindy flipped her hair over her shoulder and stomped off, dragging Camela with her.

With their departure, the stable returned to its former peaceful state. Katie always enjoyed quiet weekends like this. Most of the time the barn was in an uproar, so Katie found contentment in the times when it was still. The only noise she could hear was the munching of horses as they picked through their grass hay.

She closed her eyes and relaxed a moment, but it wasn't long before the steady four-beat rhythm of a horse's walk interrupted her thoughts. The sound got louder as it approached the barn. Katie walked to the end to see who was coming. Sometimes a groom would forget to secure a stall door, and a crafty Thoroughbred would let himself out and take a tour of the farm.

Katie was pleasantly surprised to see her best friend aboard her chestnut mare. "Jan, what are you doing here?"

Jan stopped her mare and swung down from the saddle, her boots making a crisp click on the ground. "I rode to your house to see if you wanted to take Jester out today. Your mom told me you were here." She pushed her long sandy hair back from her face and led her mare to the cross-ties.

"Yeah, everyone's gone to Portland. I'm done with the stalls. I was going to set up a couple of bales and practice using my racing whip."

Jan stopped in front of King's stall and gave him a pat. "Okay if I hang around and talk to you while you practice?"

"Sure. Maybe you can see what I'm doing wrong. I can twirl the whip when I've got the rubber band on, but I can't seem to get the hang of it on my own."

Jan helped her stack two bales of straw in the aisle, and Katie climbed on top. She didn't bother using the saddle, because she wasn't practicing for balance. She carried her whip in the down position with the popper pointed toward the ground. After several unsuccessful attempts to twirl the whip into position, she got disgusted and threw it down the shed row in a childish fit.

"What do we have here?"

Both girls' heads snapped around at the sound of the familiar male voice.

"Mark." Katie felt the blood creeping up her cheeks as she watched him stoop to pick up her discarded piece of equipment.

"Someone seems to have lost her whip," Mark said as he did a perfect twirl with the crop and cracked it across his boots, then presented it to Katie. "I presume this is yours?"

Katie's face was on fire. She hoped it didn't look as red as it felt. She grabbed the whip from his hands, lowering her eyes so she didn't have to see him laughing at her.

"There's no shame in using the rubber band, Katie," Mark admonished. "I still use it myself sometimes."

Katie could feel the rough calluses on the jockey's palms as he placed the crop into her hand. He gave her a reassuring smile that made her heart break into a trot. If Mark knew how nervous he made her, he didn't show it.

"Why don't we move forward with your lessons," Mark

suggested. "We can get you started on breaking out of the gate. That's the toughest thing to learn. The track steward will have to see you break out of the gate with several other horses before he'll give you permission to ride your two trial races."

"Trial races?" Katie asked.

Mark laughed. "You don't think they're going to turn you loose with a thousand pounds of nervous horseflesh and let you ride without first seeing if you know what you're doing?"

Once again, doubt crept into Katie's mind.

"Don't look so concerned," Mark said, playfully tugging on a lock of her hair. "It's really not *that* hard to get a license. The stewards need to see you breeze a horse in company and work a couple of horses out of the gate. If they like what they see, they give you permission to ride two trial races. If you can keep your mount out of trouble and look like you know what you're doing, then they give you an apprentice jockey's license."

Katie knew it wasn't going to be quite as easy as that.

"There's no one out on the track today," Mark said. "This will be the perfect time to get you started on the gate."

"Who will I ride?" Katie asked. "John doesn't have any of these horses scheduled to breeze until next week."

Mark looked down the row of horses. "We don't want a horse that knows how to break from the gate. That would be too fast to get you started on. I need a horse that's been on the track for a while but hasn't ever been busted out."

Katie surveyed the line of elegant Thoroughbred heads with their pointed fox ears and frowned. "The only horse here that fits that description is Willow's Destiny."

The young jockey walked up to Destiny's stall. The colt poked his nose into the middle of Mark's chest. He patted the horse and spoke softly to him. "What do you think, big guy? You sent two of us to the hospital a few days ago. Do you think you can behave today?"

Katie huffed. "You're kidding, right?"

Mark took the halter from the peg outside the stall and put it on the horse's head. "Not at all. I've ridden this horse several times. He's not a bad sort. He just got spooked the last time, and his rider didn't turn his head into the rail so he could see it. If he had, Destiny would never have gone through it."

Katie was astounded. "But what about Destiny? Won't he be too sore to ride?"

Mark nodded in agreement. "That's what makes him the perfect candidate. If his muscles are a liitle tight, he'll be too stiff to put up a fuss. John's already asked me to work the kinks out of him tomorrow, and the vet gave him a clean bill of health, so there's no problem." He looked at Katie. "Are you scared?" He paused a moment for emphasis. "A jockey can't afford to be scared. You have to ride whatever they give you. Are you sure you want to get your license?"

Katie crossed her arms and set her jaw. She wasn't about to let Mark frighten her out of this. She'd show him that she was as tough as he was. "Jan, grab the saddle. We're going to the starting gate."

⇒ Chapter Eleven ⇒

Jan handed the saddle over the stall door. "Are you crazy? This is the same horse that took a rider through the rail and came out of it without a scratch on him. That alone proves that he's fit for the devil. You *don't* have to do this, you know."

Katie positioned the saddle pad up high on the horse's withers and fit it into place. "Yes, I do." She pulled the cinch snug and took the bridle from her friend's outstretched hand. "Mark's right. When I get my license, I'll have to ride all kinds of horses. If I'm going to be a good jockey, I need to be experienced on crazy horses as well as good ones."

"Yeah, but does it have to be *this* crazy horse?" Jan said as she rolled her eyes.

Mark leaned his slim frame against the door. "There's no need to sweat the load. I've ridden this colt before. He's fine. What happened the other day was a freak accident. Besides, we're only going to trot him. Katie's a good rider. She'll be just fine."

Jan huffed, crossing her arms and looking Mark right in the eye. "Just in case, I'll be ponying her on my mare." She turned her stare on Katie. "This isn't like you. I'm not so sure that John would approve of this colt going out today. I'm going to make sure that nothing happens to either of you."

Katie heard her friend's disapproval loud and clear. Something in the back of her mind echoed that Jan was right. She ignored her better judgment and rechecked her mount's tack. "Let's go."

Jan opened the door for Katie, but not before giving her a look that said she was doing this under protest.

"I wish Jason were here to talk you out of this," said Jan.

Katie paused for a moment at the mention of his name. But before she could back out, Mark reached for Destiny's reins and pulled the colt out into the aisle.

"Well, Jason's not here, and *I'm* the one with the jockey's license anyway," Mark said as he boosted Katie into the saddle and handed her the reins. "Katie knows I wouldn't do anything to get her hurt, don't you, Kat?" He gave her an encouraging smile.

It seemed funny to hear Mark call her by the pet name Jason used, but she didn't mind. Mark was right. He knew what he was doing. She'd just have to trust him. She returned his smile. "Let's get going. The Kentucky Derby is getting closer by the minute."

"You mean the race I plan to win?" Mark said, smiling at Katie, who laughed. She had to give Mark credit for being persistent.

Jan moved her mare to the end of the barn and hooked a removable line through Destiny's bit, snugging him up close so he couldn't try any monkey business. But the colt nipped at Jan's leg. Katie popped him with her bat. He danced around for a few steps, then took his cue and settled into a nice walk.

Jan rubbed her leg. "After his last mishap, this horse shouldn't even be alive. Where does he get off biting me? I don't like this at all, Katie. And I'm beginning to have my doubts about Mark."

"But you were the one pushing for him so hard in the beginning." Katie looked around to make sure the jockey was out of earshot. "You're not being fair, Jan. He's got my best interests at heart."

"Does he?" Jan said. "You realize that *he* wants to be the one who rides Willow King in the Derby, and he's never said anything different. Do you really think he's just going to step aside and give up the *Kentucky Derby* without a fight?"

Katie didn't know what to say. Her friend was making some sense. "Of course he has my interests at heart," Katie insisted. "Why wouldn't he?" She hid her irritation in the busy movements of checking her tack and adjusting the stirrups.

"With a Derby purse worth a million dollars, and the jockey getting *ten percent* of the winner's share, why not indeed?" Jan asked pointedly.

Before Katie could respond, Mark jogged up beside them. Both girls immediately fell silent.

"I'm going to take the shortcut and get the gate ready," Mark said. "As long as you've got the pony-horse, why don't you jog Destiny around the track once to loosen him up and take the edge off."

They entered the track, and Jan clucked her mare into a trot. Katie stood in the irons and crossed her reins down low on the horse's neck. If the colt wanted to pull, he could pull against himself. After a little bit of dancing around, Destiny lined out and trotted like a well-broken horse.

"Maybe the accident took a little more out of him than we thought," Katie said.

Despite Destiny's calm manner, Jan kept a steady hold on the lead rope. "I'm gonna keep him on a short line, just in case," she said. "I don't trust this colt at all."

"Me neither," Katie agreed.

"Then why are we doing this?"

Katie shrugged. "I know you think I'm out of my mind, but this is something I've got to do. When I was younger, people babied me because of my limp. I want to *earn* my jockey's license. I want to be able to ride the rough stock just like the rest of them. I don't want to hear anybody whispering that I made it because everyone took pity on me and gave me the easy horses."

Jan nodded her head. "I understand. And as your best friend, you know I'm with you. But don't expect me not to worry. Especially when you're riding knuckleheads like this. I know you're *capable* of riding Destiny, but some things are better left alone."

They were almost back to the starting gate. Katie pulled Destiny down to a walk. "I'll be okay. But thanks for looking out for me."

"Katie!" a voice suddenly boomed from the track entrance.

"Look, Jason's here," Jan said as she waved him over.

Katie chuckled. "Why is it you sound so relieved?"

Jan pulled on the pony strap without answering, leading Katie and Destiny toward Jason.

"Hey, we're supposed to be going to the gate," Katie

said. They stopped in front of Jason, and Katie could see the disapproval in his face. Jason took his Stetson off and cocked his head, looking at Destiny and then Katie. "What are you doing on this crazy colt, Kat? Does John know you're riding this horse?"

Katie looked at the spot between Destiny's ears. She didn't want to look Jason in the eye. "Mark said it was okay," she said.

Jason plopped his hat back on his head and glanced toward the starting gate, where Mark waited. "Last time I checked, John was the trainer here," Jason said. "Mark doesn't have any right to say which horse goes out or who rides them."

Katie felt her anger flare. "John asked Mark to ride Destiny tomorrow," she informed Jason. "Mark didn't think it would hurt anything if I rode him today. I need to learn how to break out of the gate so I can get my license, and Mark says that Destiny is the best horse to do it on."

Jason shook his head. "Destiny sent two riders to the hospital the other day, Katie. And Mark was one of them. Are you sure he's not trying to get you out of the way so he can ride Willow King in the Derby?"

Katie's hands clenched on the reins. "What's wrong with everyone? Mark's just holding up his end of our bargain. I want to get my jockey's license, and that's something *you* can't help me with!"

Katie instantly regretted her harsh words when she saw the hurt look that passed over Jason's features. "Look," she said in a softer tone. "I really want to do this, Jason. Can't you just be supportive?"

Mark yelled and waved at them from the gate. "Come on back. I'm ready for you!"

Jason gave Katie an exasperated look. "I'll try, Kat, but I'm telling you now that I don't like this one bit. You shouldn't be on this colt in the gate. He's never popped out the front of it before." Jason ducked under the rail and strode toward the starting gate. "But if you insist on doing this, I'm going to be here."

Jan turned her mare and ponied Katie toward the gate.

The starting gate was placed at the back of a straight-away chute adjoining the racetrack. There was a large space behind the gate for maneuvering the animals into position. Jan pulled the lead rope from Destiny's bit, and Katie directed the horse to this warm-up area.

"I'll wait at the head of the chute in case Destiny decides he wants to act like a grown-up racehorse and run down the track," said Jan. "I'll be there to pick you up if he does."

"Thanks," Katie said as she gave Jan the thumbs-up sign, then trotted back to where Mark and Jason were waiting. She noticed that the two boys were glaring at one another. She hoped Jason hadn't given Mark a piece of his mind—she felt that she finally had a good jockey to teach her, and she didn't want to lose him.

Mark motioned Katie over to the number-four hole.

"Katie, has this colt ever seen the inside of a starting gate before?" he asked. "Has he been in here to just stand?"

"He's never been in the gate before," Jason said abruptly as he moved closer to the starting gate.

Destiny eyed the gate warily and approached it with apprehensive steps. Katie smooched and prodded him with her heels, speaking words of encouragement as he slowly advanced. "He was scheduled to start gate training next week," Katie said. "But I don't think he likes it."

Mark jumped down from the gate and grabbed the colt's chin strap. "We're just going to stand him in there to begin with. After he gets used to the sights and sounds, we'll walk him out to where Jan is waiting. Make him stop and turn in, just like you do when he pulls up after a work. Then bring him back, and we'll close the doors on him."

"Do you need any help?" Jason offered.

"Thanks," Mark said as he waved him off. "But I've got it covered."

Katie smiled nervously. "What do you want me to do when we're in there?"

"For now, just sit still and *relax*. I'll have hold of the colt's head. You'll be okay."

Mark was right, Katie thought. She had to get control of these jitters or she'd telegraph them to her mount. Destiny was crazy enough without giving him reason to be even more so. She took several deep breaths, easing her death grip on the reins. Everything was going to be great.

"Ready?" Mark said.

Katie nodded and asked the colt to move forward. Mark guided them into the gate. When they were in position, the jockey quietly climbed onto the padded shelf that served as a foothold for the gatemen.

At the racetrack, there was one gateman for every two horses. His job was to stand on the platform between each pair of horses and keep the skittish animals looking straight down the track so they'd be ready to break fast when the doors popped open. For now, Mark kept Destiny's head pulled to the side so he wouldn't be tempted to leave the gate. When the colt had stood silently for several minutes, Mark turned Destiny's head loose and asked Katie to walk him out.

The colt stepped hesitantly at first, looking to the right and left. But then he walked quietly to Jan's mare. They repeated this exercise several times until Destiny was totally at ease with the routine.

"Looks like we're ready to close the doors on him," Mark said. "Bring him on in the same way you did when the front was open."

Katie guided the colt into the starting gate with ease. "I think he's getting the hang of it."

Jason stood to the side, carefully taking in all that was happening.

"Steady, now," Mark said. "I'm going to close the rear gate so he can't back out on us. We'll let him sit in here for a moment to think about this."

The door clicked shut behind them. Destiny tensed at the sound and began flicking his ears back and forth to catch any noise that might help him figure out what was going on. Katie leaned forward and scratched his neck. "Easy, big guy. This is a piece of cake. We haven't even gotten to the tough stuff yet."

When the colt settled down, Katie straightened and turned to face Mark. "How long will it take before I can test for my jockey's license?"

Mark crossed his arms and leaned against the gate. "If we can get you up to Portland to break with four or five other horses a couple of times..." He scratched his chin, contemplating the answer. "My guess is about two weeks."

"Two weeks!" Katie about fell off her horse. "How could I possibly be ready in two weeks?" Destiny picked up on her agitation and fidgeted under her.

"Are you sure you don't want some help in there?" Jason asked, but he was quickly rebuffed by Mark. Jason gritted his teeth and held his place on the sideline.

Mark reached for the colt's reins, putting a steadying hand on Destiny's neck. He laughed at Katie. "Don't look so shocked. I've watched you quite a few times in the morning. You're good."

Katie blushed at the compliment. Hearing that from Mark gave her the confidence boost she needed.

"The only thing different between galloping in the morning and racing in the afternoon is that you're working with a lot more horses," Mark explained. "They can fit twelve in our gate at Portland, but a lot of the time you're running against fewer than that. Once you get some experience breaking out of the gate, you should be good to go."

Katie shook her head in disbelief. "But what about maneuvering around in the pack? How do you learn where to place your horse? John's always complaining about a rider getting a horse boxed in so he can't run."

Mark placed a hand on her shoulder and gave it a slight squeeze. "That, my friend, comes from experience. When the steward gives you permission to ride your first two trial races, your job is just to keep out of trouble and ride a clean race. If you can do that, you'll get your apprentice license. Then you can learn how to do the fancy stuff, like positioning your horse and boxing somebody in so their mount can't run."

Katie's head swam. She wanted her license badly, but

she'd had no idea it could happen so fast. Mark put a finger under her chin and lifted her face to meet his. "You look a little green around the gills. Are you okay?"

Jason growled from his place on the rail, and Katie gave him a look of warning before turning her attention back to Mark.

She nodded. "I'm all right. It just kind of surprises me that I could be riding in the races so soon. What if I mess up? What if I cause a wreck?"

Mark ruffled her hair. "Those are the things you try not to worry about. This is a dangerous sport. You've got a hundred-pound rider racing around the track on an excited thousand-pound animal doing a little over thirty miles per hour. The only protection you have is your helmet."

Katie was silent for a moment. She let out a low whistle. "That's a good recipe for disaster."

"This is a fun job, but it's not for the weak at heart," he warned. "My friend used to say, *'When you're sliding to the ground with a thousand pounds of horseflesh on top of you, it's hard to remember that your first objective was to win the race.'*"

Katie laughed. "That puts it all in perspective. What's your friend doing now?"

Mark grew serious. "He's in a wheelchair. The horse he was riding went down at the front of the pack. Five horses went over the top of him. The sixth one stepped in the middle of his back."

Katie's breath caught in her throat and her mind reeled. "I'm sorry. I had no idea."

"It's okay." He shrugged his shoulders. "He's learning to live with it. Unfortunately, that kind of accident is a possibility every time you climb on one of these guys," Mark said as he patted Destiny's neck. He looked Katie square in the eye. "If you're having doubts, Katie, know your mind *now*. Don't wait until you're in the middle of your first race to freak out. That's how riders get hurt...and sometimes killed."

"Are you trying to scare me?" she said as her spine stiffened, refusing to break eye contact.

"Yes, I am. There's no room for wimps in this business. Everybody has to pull their own weight."

Anger burned in her chest. Her hands tightened on the reins, and Destiny pawed at the ground. "Are you insinuating that I can't pull my share of the load? Is that because I'm a girl with a weak leg?"

Mark laughed and clapped her on the back. "Geez, Katie, lighten up. I was only testing you." He gave her a wry grin. "But I should warn you. There are a lot of guys who don't like women jockeys. They think you're not strong enough to control your mounts."

Katie gave a small tug on Destiny's bit, straightening his head and getting him back under control. "What about you? How do you feel about women riders?"

"They don't bother me," Mark said. "In fact, I think women have better hands than a lot of guys. And I think that's why some of the guys don't like women riders. They just don't want to be shown up."

Katie squared her shoulders. "Whether they like me or not, they're going to have to live with it, because I'm not giving up."

"That's the spirit." Mark jumped down, stood in front of the gate, and unhitched the latch. "This guy's been standing in here long enough. Let's get both of you started on your road to success."

Mark opened the doors and quickly stepped out of the way. Destiny pricked his ears, staring at the sudden expanse of racetrack that lay ahead of him. Katie smooched and tapped him with her heels. The colt paused for a second longer, then took several steps from the gate, breaking into a trot once he was clear.

"Great!" Mark yelled. "Bring him back and we'll do it one more time." He turned to Jason and smiled. "She's a natural."

Jason didn't return the smile.

Katie pulled Destiny up near Jan's mare, looking back over her shoulder. "Don't you think he's had enough for today?" Jan asked Mark. "This colt has an awfully short attention span."

"Just once more," Mark promised. "We haven't asked that much of him."

Jan rolled her eyes. "The master has spoken. Let's get this over with and go to my house for lunch."

Jason stepped behind the gate. "I agree with Jan," he said. "I think Destiny has had enough for today."

Mark looked Jason up and down, seeming to size him up. Judging from the look, it seemed he didn't like what he saw. "We can stop after this next time out of the gates," Mark said defiantly.

Katie turned Willow's Destiny around and posted at a trot back to the gate. "You're on," she said to Mark.

This time when they entered the gate, Destiny was acting very eager. He chomped at the bit and pawed at the ground, wanting to be off.

"Easy, boy," Katie crooned. "We'll be out of here in no

time, and you'll be back eating your oats."

"I think he's got the idea," Mark said as he prepared to unlatch the gate. "This time I'm going to let them flop open. They make quite a bit of noise when they do, so get tied on."

"What do you mean, *tied on?*" Katie rattled the colt's bit, trying to keep his mind in the right place. Destiny shook his head and pawed at the dirt, wanting to run down the track.

Jason poked his head over the gate. "Would you like me to come up there and be your gateman, Katie? Destiny looks like he's getting pretty antsy. I know this colt—when he gets like this, he starts trouble."

Mark gave Jason a dirty look. "Katie's a big girl," he wisecracked. "She can handle this horse." He turned his attention back to Katie, giving Jason his back.

Mark grabbed a handful of Destiny's mane up high on the neck. "Getting *tied on* means hanging on up here so you don't fall off if your horse comes bolting out of the gate," he said. "Keep a rein in each hand, with a little slack in them so you don't hit the horse's mouth when he breaks, and lean forward. If you're sitting too upright, the force of the break will set you way back in the saddle. I've seen riders topple off the rear of the horse."

Destiny's nervousness passed on to Katie. She could feel the dampness in her palms and hear the thud of her heartbeat. She grabbed a fistful of mane.

"Put a little more slack in your reins," Mark instructed. "You don't want him to hit the bit and stop running as soon as he breaks. Give him plenty of slack. Then, after you're out of the gate, set your rein where you want it."

Katie took a calming breath, but it had no effect. She

had to get control of herself. Her shaking hands were telegraphing her thoughts to Destiny, and he was acting worse by the moment. She looked to Jason, and he gave her an encouraging, although forced, smile. She breathed a little easier, but she knew Destiny was almost at the end of his patience. "Better get us out of here. He feels like he's ready to blow," Katie said.

"Sit tight–let me work this latch. It could use a good oiling," Mark said, looking pointedly at Jason.

Katie readjusted her hold on Destiny's neck and hung on for dear life, praying she'd be able to stay on if the horse decided to break and run instead of repeating the trot they had been practicing.

Destiny stilled for a moment, seeming to sense that something big was about to happen. When the gate didn't open, he shifted backward, running into the tail door and shaking the entire gate. The sound of metal clanging against metal echoed in their ears as Katie felt the colt's front feet come off the ground in a series of little hops.

"Dang, I can't get this latch open," Mark said between clenched teeth. "Hold him still in there, Kat. You're not helping matters."

Jason came around the side of the gate to help, but Mark waved him back with a flip of his hand.

Katie felt Destiny shift beneath her and knew that she was in trouble, but things happened so fast, she barely had time to react. Destiny bolted against the front of the gate, hitting the steel doors. The impact was hard enough to knock Mark backward into the sand. The doors still remained shut. Destiny reared high into the air, pawing at the doors and causing a terrible racket.

The sound of metal against metal shrieked into the air again as the horse's aluminum shoes clanged against the doors. Destiny reared, going higher and higher into the air. Then he began to falter backward. Out of the corner of her eye, Katie saw Jason running forward, but she knew he wouldn't get there fast enough to save her.

"No!" Katie screamed as Destiny tumbled over, losing his footing and slamming down against the back of the gate.

Katie pulled her feet from the irons and released the reins as the two of them fell, but she couldn't get clear of the horse. When the dust settled, Destiny lay almost upside down against the gate, like a baby in his mother's arms.

Katie flattened her arms against the stall space, trying not to slide any farther down the divider. One of her legs was trapped between the terrified horse and the wall. Destiny's front hoof was almost parallel to her face. She prayed that for once in his life, the colt wouldn't panic and start thrashing about. If he did, she was dead.

⇒ *Chapter Twelve* ⇒

Jason's and Mark's eyes peeked over the top of the gate. Jan kept her mare down the track so she wouldn't upset Destiny further, causing him to panic and struggle.

"Don't move," Jason whispered.

Mark nodded his head in agreement.

Move? Katie thought. She was scared to even breathe.

"I'm going to sneak around to the back and unlatch the tail door," Jason said. "I'm not going to lie, Katie. This is going to be tricky." He gave Mark a harsh look, then surveyed the problem in tight-lipped silence.

Mark signaled silently with his hands to get Jason's attention. "I think I can get her out of here," he said.

Jason turned his piercing blue eyes, nailing Mark to the spot. "Don't even think about it," he said in a low, menacing voice. Jason quickly turned his attention back to Katie. "Here's what we're going to do, Kat. Without moving anything but your eyes, see if you think you can reach the top of the divider wall and pull yourself clear when I let this horse out."

Katie strained her eyes, looking to the edge of her

vision. Cold droplets of sweat ran down her brow. She blinked hard as the salty drops burned into her pupils. The lip of the wall was only inches above her outstretched hand, but the space could have been a mile.

Destiny groaned, and she knew it was only a matter of moments before he began to struggle. She stared at the large hoof that was level with her face. It moved in a rhythmic sway with each heaving breath the colt took. It didn't matter that the gap between her fingers and the edge of the gate seemed as wide as the Grand Canyon. She knew she had to make it.

She breathed in the heavy smell of horse sweat and signaled to Jason with the slightest inclination of her head that she could do it.

Destiny slid a little farther down the gate, putting more pressure on Katie's trapped leg. He still hadn't tried to move, but she could see the whites of his eyes as they rolled in his head. It wouldn't be long before he threw a full-fledged fit. She couldn't believe that he hadn't already.

Jason motioned to Mark as he moved to the rear of the gate. "We're going to get one shot at this," he said. "When I release this door, Katie's going to have to grab for that edge and pull herself out. Mark, you help her any way you can." He paused for a moment, trying to sound brave for Katie's sake. "Katie, you need to reach that lip. If you miss, you won't get a second chance."

Katie winced as Destiny took a deep breath and let out a frightened whinny. The sound was deafening as it ricocheted off the steel walls and reverberated inside her head. Then Destiny's whinny was answered by Jan's mare.

For a moment the colt was motionless; he even ceased

to breathe. In that millisecond, Katie heard the metallic click of the door latch. Destiny called again and immediately struggled for freedom.

Katie felt a sharp pain as the colt's hoof grazed her face. She desperately reached for the edge of the wall, straining to get her fingers over the lip of it. Destiny's foot passed in front of her eyes, slamming into the wall beside her. Her grip loosened as she tried to pull free of the horse's weight. She felt Mark's hand grab for her, but he missed.

Destiny toppled backward out of the gate, screaming in terror and flinging his head from side to side. Katie felt the pressure drop from her pinned leg, but her relief was short-lived, as the colt caught her in the midsection with his head.

The air exploded from her lungs. Her palms slipped from the wall, scraping over the hard metal edge. She was falling, and there was nothing she could do.

Suddenly, strong fingers closed over her forearm and held tight, jerking her up short. She cried out at the burning pain that racked her arm as Jason's hands dug into her flesh, pulling her to safety.

Willow's Destiny cleared the gate and scrambled to his feet, his eyes wide with terror. Mark grabbed his reins and comforted the colt, checking him for injury.

Jason released Katie's arms, and her feet hit the ground. She bent over with her hands on her knees, drawing in great gulps of air. Her entire body shook.

Jan rushed up on her mare, flying out of the saddle before the mare even stopped. "Are you okay?" She laid a steadying hand on Katie's shoulder.

Katie couldn't find her voice, so she nodded her head. At least she *thought* she was all right. She couldn't be sure until she got her breath back and could move around. Katie prayed that the pressure on her leg hadn't knocked her hips out of alignment again.

Jason placed a comforting hand on Katie's back and brushed the hair off her damp forehead. "You gave us quite a scare. You sure you're all right?"

Mark led Destiny to within a few feet of the gate. "Are you hurt?" he asked Katie.

Katie slowly uprighted herself and flexed her joints. They popped and crackled, but everything seemed to be in working order. "I think I'm okay. How about Destiny?"

"He's got a cut on his front leg. Nothing that needs stitches, though."

"Great," Katie said as she rubbed the abrasion on her forehead. It stung like crazy, but she didn't think she'd have to see the doctor for it. "What are we going to tell John?"

"We're not going to tell him anything," Mark said defensively. "With any luck, he'll think Destiny banged himself up in the stall."

Katie shook her head in disbelief. "I can't lie to him. He's the trainer. He has to know what's going on. I don't want somebody else to get hurt on this colt."

Jason stepped in front of Katie. "I'm the assistant trainer, Kat. Let me handle this." He walked to where Mark stood, straightening to his full height in front of the jockey. "Isn't it bad enough that Katie almost got killed?" Jason said as he grabbed Destiny's reins from Mark's hand. "I only went along with this because Katie asked me to stay out of it. But you've gone too far, Mark. You had no right to take this colt out today. Next time you have to ask permission. And leave Katie out of the dangerous stuff!"

Katie massaged her sore back as she watched the exchange take place. She didn't like the way this was going. Jason looked as if he was ready to tackle Mark. "I better go break this up," she said to Jan.

Katie hobbled over to where the boys stood. She thought they looked like two raging bulls, ready to lock horns in battle. She laid her hand gently on Jason's arm. "He didn't know I was going to get hurt, Jason. It was an accident."

Katie was surprised by the incredulity she saw on Jason's face when he turned to her.

"You're defending him?" Jason said in shock.

Katie shrugged her shoulders. "I'm not really *defending* him, I just don't want you to blame Mark for all of this. I had a part in it too. I should have known better than to get on Destiny in the gate. I should have listened to you." She attempted a smile, hoping Jason would understand. But Jason just shook his head and walked off, clearly not understanding at all.

"John's going to hear about this," Jason tossed back at Mark as he walked the colt off the track. "Don't be making decisions around here that aren't *yours* to make!"

"Fine!" Mark yelled back at him. "You'll get us all fired, and then who will teach Katie?" Mark looked at Katie and huffed, "You better get that guy under control." Then he turned and stomped off the track.

Jan gathered her mare and offered Katie a ride back to the barn. "Looks like Prince Charming might have a few dents in his armor."

Katie stood on the edge of the gate and slid onto the mare's back. "I'm beginning to see what you mean."

*   *   *

Katie's mother made *tsk*ing sounds as she drew Katie a hot bath. "I agree with Jason," Mrs. Durham said. "Mark had no right to put you on that colt without the trainer's permission. If he doesn't have any more sense than that, maybe you should see about getting another teacher."

Katie smiled gratefully at her mother for drawing the bath, but she kept her mouth closed on the subject of Mark. As she relaxed in the hot water, her mind went over all the details of the starting gate catastrophe. The more she thought about it, the more she realized how wrong she had been to let Mark talk her into it.

It was a good thing Jason had been there to save her, Katie thought. Who knew what might have happened if he hadn't followed them out to the gate? One thing was sure—they were going to have to tell John about this. Katie frowned at the thought. She hoped this wouldn't destroy the trust the old trainer had in her. She sank deeper into the hot bath, promising herself that the next time Mark asked her to do something crazy, she would listen to her better judgment.

The following morning, Katie told John about Destiny's accident in the gate. John was disappointed that she would go along with such a plan, but he decided to forgive her. Mark, however, got a half-hour lecture on using his common sense. When John felt that the message had sunk in, he allowed Mark to stay on as Willow Run's jockey.

At first Mark was angry with Katie for telling John about the accident. Katie worried that it might mean the end of her jockey lessons. But eventually Mark forgave her, and soon he was back to teaching her how to break from the starting gate. This time they worked with well-trained horses.

Katie could tell that Jason still hadn't forgiven Mark for taking such a big chance with her safety. It showed in the way he scowled every time Mark walked down the shed row. Katie tried to maintain the peace, but it was uncomfortable every time the two boys were together. She hoped that in time they would forget about it. Everyone needed to work as a team if they were to get Willow King to the Kentucky Derby.

By the end of the week, the tension had somewhat lessened, and everyone fell into the regular routine. One day after school, Katie was working Cousin Millie out of the starting gate with Mark and another horse, and she beat him to the finish line. When they pulled the horses up, Mark looked at her with a wide grin and broke the news.

"I think you're ready to go to Portland and ride with the big boys," he said as they walked through the exit gate.

"Do you really think so?" Katie reached out and patted Cousin Millie on the neck.

"Yes. You're one-hundred-percent improved since the first time you did a fast break and almost fell off the back of the horse," Mark teased.

"That wasn't much fun," Katie said, laughing. "But I just don't *feel* ready. I don't think I know enough yet. I watched you ride the other day, and you won four out of five races. When I think about competing against you, it makes my stomach turn over."

Mark turned his mount toward the barn. "You know as much as you need to for getting started. The rest of it you can only get in the races. You need experience under your belt. I know you've got thoughts about riding King in the Derby, but it takes time to become a good jockey. It wouldn't be fair to King if he got less than a perfect ride in such a big race."

Katie didn't like the way this conversation was turning. There was no doubt that Mark had a lot more experience than she did. But she *knew* King, and he trusted her. King would give her everything he had to give. Wouldn't that make up for her lack of experience?

"I know you've got your heart set on riding King in the Derby, Mark. But we made a deal, and you knew that some-day I'd want to ride King."

Mark nodded. "Yes, I know that, but I think it's too early for you to think about riding in this big of a race." He unsnapped his helmet strap and kicked his feet out of the irons. "We're talking about the *Kentucky Derby,* Katie. It's one of the biggest horse races in the world! Didn't you see yesterday's article in the *Daily Racing Form* saying that King was the longest shot in the race? He needs all the help he can get."

Katie felt butterflies swirling in her stomach. Maybe Mark was right. Was she ready to ride in front of a crowd of more than a hundred thousand people? Could she control her nervousness enough to give King a good ride?

When they reached the barn, Jason came out to receive the two horses.

"By the way, Katie," Mark said, ignoring Jason as he jumped to the ground and loosened the saddle, "I know you call Willow King *your* horse, but he really belongs to your mom, doesn't he?"

Katie was taken aback. Why would he think King

belonged to her mother? Didn't he think she was responsible enough to own a horse of that caliber? "Of course he's mine." She looked to Jason for backup.

"Now, hold on," Mark said, raising his hands in mock surrender. "Don't go getting insulted. I just figured that with such an expensive type of animal, your mom probably owned him."

"I paid for him myself by working here at Willow Run," Katie said defensively.

Jason pulled the saddle from Millie's back. "If it wasn't for Katie, this horse would be planted out behind the barn under the rosebushes."

"Well, then, you've got a big problem if you want to ride King in the Derby," Mark said. "A jockey can't own a horse. It's considered a conflict of interest because he could ride someone else's horse and do a poor job of it. You'll have to put him in your mother's name or you won't be able to get a license."

Katie's heart nearly stopped. Not own King? The thought of it made her queasy.

"You okay, Kat?" Jason put a hand on her shoulder.

She nodded her head, but the words didn't want to form on her tongue.

"It's no big deal," Mark said. "He'll still be yours, but he'll be in your mother's name. I think you can trust her not to run off with him," he added, laughing.

Katie knew he was right, but her selfish pride wanted to have King in her own name. She was the one who'd had faith in him and seen him through all the rough times. She wanted to get credit for the good times they were having now.

Jason handed Mark's gelding to one of the grooms and then hooked Cousin Millie into the cross-ties. He reached into the bucket of warm water and squeezed the sponge onto Millie's sweaty back. "What are you going to do? If you want to ride, you're going to have to put King in your mother's name. How bad do you want this?"

Katie walked to King's stall and coaxed him away from his hay. He put his head over the door and stared at her with his large brown eyes. She stroked his whiskered muzzle and scratched him on the neck.

"I don't know," she said as she breathed in the warm smell of her horse. "Every night I dream about riding him in the Kentucky Derby. But to make that dream come true, I'll have to give him up."

"You're not really losing him, Kat. It's only on paper," Jason said. "Everyone knows he's your horse."

Mark joined her at Willow King's stall. "You better make a decision soon. John wants to take some colts to Portland this week. If we can get you okayed out of the gate, you could be riding your two trial races this weekend."

Now she really did feel sick. What was she going to do? "Can you finish up here?" she asked Jason. "I'm going to go home and think about this. I'll let you know what I want to do in the morning."

"Sure, Kat. I'll see you tomorrow," said Jason. "You can call me later if you want to talk."

Mark walked Katie to the end of the barn. "You've been a great student, Katie, but I'll understand if you don't want to sign King over to someone else and you decide not to become a jockey. You know I'll ride King for you anytime."

Katie looked into his smiling face. "I know you will,

Mark. Thanks..." *I think.* Katie suddenly began to get the feeling that he would be *very* happy if she chose not to get her jockey's license. She turned and walked from the stable. She had a lot of soul-searching to do.

Katie passed through a rough night of sleeplessness and then a tough day at school. But by the time she reached the barn, she had made up her mind to put King in her mother's name. The only problem was, nobody was there to share the news. She knew Jason wouldn't be here today. He had some horses to haul for his dad. But she had expected to see Mark and Camela.

When she entered the shed row, all the horses poked their heads over the doors and nickered a greeting. All of them but King. Katie smiled. He was probably stretched out on the straw catching an afternoon nap. She hoped he was enjoying his break. His wound had almost healed, and the stitches were coming out tomorrow. Then it would be back to a heavy training schedule to make up for the time he had missed.

"Come on, you lazy bum," she called as she picked up a halter and lead rope. But when she got to King's stall, she noticed that the lock wasn't latched. King wasn't in his stall.

Katie stood with her hand on the door, her mind spinning wildly, trying to remember if John had said anything about taking King to the vet's office. She shook her head— she would definitely remember something like that.

She made a quick check of the other stalls to see if one of the grooms had moved King to an empty stall while his was being cleaned and simply forgotten to put him back.

King wasn't in any of the stalls.

Katie pushed aside thoughts of horse theft in favor of the theory of an escapee. Someone must have left the colt's door unlatched, and King had figured out how to open it. Had Camela forgotten to snap the lock after she had poured feed, or missed the latch because she couldn't see it?

The sound of a nicker drew Katie's attention. She walked out of the barn and around the corner. In the grassy section at the edge of the stables where all the sick horses grazed during their recovery stood King, munching away on the green shoots of spring grass.

"Oh, no," Katie groaned as she walked quickly to King's side. "Easy, easy. How long have you been grazing here, silly boy?" Katie looped the lead rope around King's neck to hold him in place while she slipped the halter over his head. She pulled the remaining blades of grass from King's lips. "Don't you know that only sick horses graze on this stretch of grass?" she scolded. Her mind whirled. They had missed the Jim Beam, and now the Santa Anita Derby was only nine days away. King had already missed a week of training because of his shoulder wound. He couldn't afford to miss any more time between now and the Derby.

King stretched his neck, pulling Katie back toward the grass. She jerked him up short and turned him toward the barn.

Camela was waiting in the shed row when they turned the corner. Katie saw the eager look on the girl's face and felt a heaviness in her heart. Camela wanted to help and was so proud of her new accomplishments. Did Katie dare hand her a setback? But if it had been Camela who left the door open, something would have to be said. What if King had run down the roadway and hurt himself?

"I was just here fifteen minutes ago to give the horses their afternoon grain," Camela said. "I didn't know you were taking one of them for a walk."

Katie hesitated for a moment before she asked, "Has Jason, John, or anyone else been here today?"

Camela shook her head. "Just me so far."

"Oh, Camela," Katie sighed. "King's door wasn't latched. He got out and was wandering around."

The smile dropped from Camela's face. "Is he okay?"

Katie returned King to his stall and removed his halter. "He's all right, but when I found him, he was out eating where the sick horses usually graze. I think he'll be okay, though."

Camela covered her face with her hands. "I blew it," she squeaked. "King's going to get sick and it'll be all my fault."

Katie put her arm around Camela's shoulders and walked her to the tack room. "It's okay, Camela. It happens to all of us. I've forgotten to check the stall doors and horses have gotten out. Remember, we don't know that King will get sick," she assured her friend.

But as Katie double-checked King's stall latch, she felt a smidgen of doubt creep into her mind. Things had been going wrong around the barn lately. Would King really be all right? Or would he fall prey to their recent streak of bad luck?

⇥ *Chapter Thirteen* ⇤

"Come on, Katie girl, the horses are loaded and ready to go!" called John as he revved the pickup's engine.

Jason winked at Katie as he grabbed her helmet and whip from their pegs on the wall. "I think John's about to take off without you," he teased. "Good thing your mother's in the truck or he would've left by now."

Katie took the riding equipment from Jason's hands and smiled nervously. She had received permission to miss her morning classes so that she could go to Portland and ride in front of the stewards. She was so nervous that she felt she was going to be sick. "Are you sure you can't go?" she pleaded with Jason. He shook his head and reminded her that John had left him in charge of the stable during his absence.

A noise at the tack room door startled Katie. She turned to see who it was. Mark stood there with a single spring daisy held in his hand. Her eyes cut quickly to Jason, who was frowning.

"I wanted to catch you before you left, to wish you good luck," Mark said, handing her the flower.

"Thanks." Katie took the flower and put it in her

unfinished glass of water, almost tipping it over as her shirt sleeve caught on a leaf. "I'm feeling pretty nervous right now," she apologized. The horn blared again, and Katie grabbed her things. "Sorry, I've got to go. I'll call you guys later and let you know how it went." She ran down the aisle to catch her ride, not daring to look back and see if Jason and Mark were at each other's throats.

Mrs. Durham pushed open the door to let Katie into the truck. "You look a little pale. Are you going to be okay?" she asked.

Katie climbed in and shut the door. "Yes, I'll be fine. I've just got a bad case of nerves." Her stomach rumbled in protest. She hadn't been able to eat anything this morning.

"Katie," John began in a fatherly tone, "this isn't a life-or-death matter. The world won't come to an end if you don't pass today. Everyone knows you're a very good rider, and you'll be a great jockey. If you don't make it today, we'll come back next week, and the week after that if that's how long it takes you to get up your confidence. You *will* get your license. It's just up to you how long you want it to take."

Katie leaned back into the seat cushion and stared at the truck's roof. The old trainer was right. She knew what she was doing. Mark had given her good instruction. She just needed to block everyone else out and do what she knew how to do. What was it Camela had said? *There's no need to fear the wind if your haystacks are tied down.*

She turned to John and smiled. "Thanks. I needed to hear that. Now, can I have one of those doughnuts? I'm starving."

The track was bustling with activity when they arrived.

Grooms washed hot horses and snapped them to the hot-walker to cool out, while jockeys and exercise riders ran to catch their next mounts.

Katie pulled Cousin Millie and one of the farm's older geldings from the trailer and put them in holding stalls.

John plopped the tack on a saddle rack outside the door. "I'm going to tell the stewards we're here. You get these horses groomed, and throw the tack on the old horse first. I'll be back in a few."

Katie entered the gelding's stall. Road Runner was his registered name, but everyone called him Ralph. She ran the soft brush over his chestnut coat, marveling at the way it gleamed like a new penny.

He was the perfect horse for today. The grooms called him the "baby-sitter" because of the way he took care of young riders. Jason swore he had seen the old horse run sideways down the track once to stay under a rider who had lost his balance and was tipping off the side.

"You'll take care of me, won't you, old boy?" She offered the gelding a slice of apple. "There's plenty more where that came from if we pull this off today."

Katie finished tacking the horse, then tied him to the ring in the wall and went outside to wait for John. The trainer returned in a few minutes with the news.

"Get your helmet on," John said. "They're going to meet us at the gate in ten minutes. One of the gatemen said they're okaying a lot of young stock today, so there should be plenty of company for you to go with out of the gate."

"You can do this, honey." Mrs. Durham smiled. "Just take a deep breath and relax."

Katie returned her mother's smile, then put on her gear

and accepted John's leg up on the horse. She knotted her reins and adjusted the stirrups while the trainer led them to the track entrance.

"I want you to trot this old boy around the track once to get him warmed up. He can give those colts a good lesson in breaking from the gate." John slapped the horse on the rump. "Now show 'em what you got, Katie girl!"

Katie backtracked the gelding for a short way, then turned him to the rail before trotting off. They circled the racecourse once for a warm-up, then walked back to the starting gate. She recognized the wiry steward who stood beside the gate. He had once been a jockey. This was the same man who had given her a gallop license. She felt some of the tension ease out of her shoulders. "Good morning, Mr. Palmer," Katie said.

"Morning, missy. You ready to hit the big time?" He shifted his spectacles and took his position on the rail at the front of the gate. "Just do like you normally do," the steward instructed. "I'm not impressed with anything fancy. All I care about is safety. You show me you can ride without being a danger to yourself or anyone else, and I'll give you a ticket to ride a few races."

Katie smiled and nodded. She liked Mr. Palmer's no-nonsense approach to things. She directed Ralph to the waiting area behind the gate. Several colts had already been loaded in. One of the gatemen took the old gelding by the cheek strap and guided him into the stall. Then he stood on the platform and waited while two other horses were being loaded.

"Going for your license today, huh?" asked the dark-haired kid.

Katie nodded and took a deep breath.

"Don't worry, I'll make sure your horse's head is straight and you get a good start. Just keep your eye on the other horses when you get out there. There's some youngsters in this batch, and sometimes they tend to break sideways."

The boy must have seen the panic in Katie's eyes, because he was quick to reassure her.

"Don't worry yourself none. Just get out fast and leave them in the dust. You'll be fine."

Katie smiled her thanks. Her mouth was so dry that she couldn't form any words.

"Everyone ready?" the starter called from the platform at the side of the gate.

The colt in the stall next to Katie took a sudden step backward, bumping into the rear doors and causing the entire gate to shake. Ralph pricked his ears but remained steady, staring down the racetrack. The gateman shook the colt's rein and pointed his nose back into the center of the gate.

"All clear," the starter yelled. "Get tied on!" he added as he pushed the start button.

Katie grabbed a handful of mane up high, the way Mark had taught her. She heard the bell ring at the same moment the gate clanged open. Ralph didn't need any urging. He surged forward, his powerful hindquarters pushing off with tremendous strength. They cleared the gate and shot to the front of the pack.

Katie looked back over her left shoulder, making sure the way was clear before moving her horse over to the rail. She kept her body low over Ralph's withers. Another horse moved up to challenge them, but Katie kept her mount steady and waited for the push down the homestretch.

When they hit the top of the stretch, Katie asked Ralph for more speed. The old gelding surged forward. The rider next to her went for his whip, pushing his mount to keep up with them, but Ralph continued to pull away. He crossed the finish line a full length ahead of his challenger—and several lengths ahead of the pack.

Katie repeated the drill with Cousin Millie twenty minutes later. But just as the gateman had warned, one of the colts came out crooked and slammed right into them. She felt her horse's body being pushed to the side. She steadied the mare until Millie righted her balance and began to move forward.

This time Katie found herself at the back of the pack and had to work her way up. She finished second out of five horses. The steward was sufficiently impressed to give her the okay for two trial races.

"I can't believe it!" Katie told John and her mother on their way back to Salem. "I get to ride in real races!"

John handed Katie and her mother sandwiches and sodas he had purchased from the track's kitchen. "How does this Saturday sound for your first real race?" he asked.

Katie had just taken a drink of her soft drink when John's question registered. She choked on the gulp and had a coughing fit. Her mother patted her on the back while John laughed heartily. "You did expect to actually *ride* in races, didn't you?" he asked. "Or were you just going to frame the license and hang it on the wall?"

Katie pulled a tissue from the glove box. "It's just all happening so fast, I haven't really had time to think about anything. But of course I'm expecting to ride!"

"Good." John pulled the truck and trailer out into traffic. "Cause I've got Millie entered in the fourth race on Saturday and Road Runner in the fifth on Sunday. I'd like *you* to ride them."

Katie swallowed hard, but this time her mouth was full of sandwich. The bite of ham and Swiss felt like a bowling ball going down her throat. She nodded. "This is what I've been waiting for. I guess I'll *have* to be ready."

When they reached Salem, John pulled the truck to a stop in front of Katie's school. She jumped out, waved to John and her mother, and ran toward the building. *It's going to be a long week,* she thought as she made her way to class.

Saturday soon arrived, and Katie was sitting in a chair on the back side of the racetrack while Camela fussed with her hair.

"I can't believe it," Camela said as she ran her fingers through Katie's hair, tying it into a French braid. Cousin Millie stuck her head over the receiving stall door and pushed her muzzle into Katie's hair. Camela jumped but then laughed and pushed the filly away. "This is hard enough without your help," she admonished the horse.

Katie grinned. She had discovered that Cam had a wonderful gift with hair. Even though Camela always wore her own locks tied back in a sloppy ponytail, she was very good at braiding somebody else's. Camela insisted that Katie's hair should be perfect for her first race. Katie didn't bother to point out that her hair would be under a helmet the entire time.

"I can't believe it," Katie said. "I have to report to the jockeys' room in thirty minutes, so I guess it must be real."

Camela pulled another lock of hair from the side of Katie's head and wove it into the pattern. "Why so early? You don't ride until the fourth race."

Katie winced as Camela pulled a little too hard on one curl. "Everyone has to weigh in and get their gear in order. Plus, I don't think they want us fraternizing with the crowd. People have this crazy idea that races are fixed. It's better if we're separated from the public. That removes some of the suspicion."

Camela finished the hairstyle while Katie choked down the rest of her lunch.

"Stay out in front so this hairdo doesn't get all muddy," Camela said as she patted Katie's hair. "It rained all night, so the track is probably a mess."

Katie laughed. "Jason says Millie's got enough speed to get out front and stay there. If that's true, I won't get dirty at all. Your braid will be fresh enough to wear to our pizza party tonight."

Just as Katie was finishing her salad, Jason arrived to take her to the front side of the track. "Well, it looks like this is it," said Katie as she stood and brushed imaginary lint from her shirt. "Wish me luck, Cam."

Camela gave her a big hug. "You don't need luck, Katie—you've got talent. I'll see you in the winner's circle."

Katie could feel the stares of the male riders as she walked up the steps to the jockeys' room. She smiled at some of the guys she recognized, then pushed through the door to the women's quarters. There was only one other jockey in the room. She was a pretty blond with a friendly smile. Katie guessed her to be about eighteen.

"Hi, I'm Nancy," said the jockey as she extended her hand. "You must be the new girl, Katie."

Katie nodded and gripped the girl's hand. "Nice to meet you. Where should I put my stuff?" The rider pointed to a spot behind her, and Katie saw a locker that already had her name on it.

"I knew you were coming," Nancy said. "They told me you were brand-new, and I remembered what it was like the first time I rode a race."

Katie opened the locker and was surprised to find a bottle of water, several pieces of fruit, and some extra pairs of racing goggles. She turned to look at Nancy.

The jockey shrugged her shoulders and smiled. "I figured you might not remember to bring some things, so I took the liberty..."

"Thanks a lot, Nancy. I really appreciate that."

The jockey pulled on red racing silks and picked up her whip. "You've got a little while. You can borrow one of my books to pass the time. I'm in the first two races, but I'm gonna stick around to watch you ride. I want to help with the jockey's initiation if you win."

"The what?" Katie asked.

"Never mind," Nancy said as she fit a helmet onto her head and smiled. "Hopefully, you'll find out."

Then she turned and walked out the door, leaving Katie a bit confused. Katie picked up a book but couldn't concentrate. So she put on her racing silks, then slipped out the back door to an area where the jockeys could sit and watch the races. When the call came for *riders up,* she just about jumped out of her skin.

Mark was waiting by the door when she opened it to

leave. He was scheduled to ride in the sixth race.

"Hey, Katie. I just wanted to wish you good luck in your first race. And don't forget what I told you about breaking out of that gate. Millie's got a lot of speed—just get out front and keep her there. She should win this thing by at least ten lengths."

Katie smiled her thanks and moved with the rest of the riders to the paddock area. *Ten lengths? Is Mark trying to psyche me out?* Katie wondered. She entered stall number four and patted Millie on the hip. The filly shook her head and stomped hard with her back foot. Katie jumped aside, her heart racing. In all the excitement, she had forgotten that Millie was a kicker. It was a good thing the horse was feeling generous or Katie might have been going to the hospital instead of the starting gate.

Jason suddenly pulled on Katie's braid, trying to distract her from her nervousness. "John's out waiting for you on the pony-horse. He'll give you your orders during the post parade, but I know what he's going to say."

"What's that?"

"Win." Jason laughed as he legged her up and led her out to John. "Good luck, Kat. This is your moment. Enjoy it."

Katie squinted against the sun's glare as they came out from the cover of the paddock. Despite the bright rays, the track hadn't dried out from last night's downpour. It slopped beneath the horses' hooves as they entered the post parade.

"Come on, number four!" someone yelled from the stands.

"Go get 'em, Katie. Show 'em how it's done!"

Katie recognized the last voice as Camela's. She searched the crowd for her friend and spotted her jumping up and down by the rail next to her uncle and Katie's mother. *This one's for you and your grandpa, Cam,* Katie thought as she trotted past.

"Hang on. Here we go," John said as he moved them into a canter and headed for the gate. "Just get this mare out of the gate and keep her out of trouble. She'll do the rest."

Katie nodded. The starting gate loomed ahead. Her stomach was doing somersaults, and her heart felt as if it was jumping out of her chest. John pulled the horses to a walk.

This was it. It was time.

The trainer handed her over to the gate crew and took his place beside the other pony riders in back of the gate. "You'll do fine, Katie girl. Just ride like you always do," he said encouragingly.

Katie felt her lips stick to her teeth when she tried to smile. They loaded her into the four hole. She looked around at the other riders, wondering if they were nervous about having a new rider racing with them.

"Your goggles," one of the jockeys yelled above the noise of the shouting gatemen and snorting horses. "Don't forget to pull your goggles down."

"Thanks," Katie said as she pulled the protective eyeware into place. Thank goodness the rider had reminded her. Without goggles, the splattering mud would have made it very hard to see. Katie reached up to pat Millie, trying to calm the filly down. She only succeeded in making her more nervous.

"They're all in," a gateman hollered as he stepped across the stall dividers, trying to reach an unruly colt.

Millie bounced against the gate, and Katie's heart caught in her throat. A gateman grabbed the side of Millie's bridle and straightened her head, forcing the filly to look down the track. Katie grabbed a handful of mane and said her prayers.

"Get tied on!" the gateman called.

Katie had only a second to think before the bell rang and the gates popped open, sending all ten horses and riders racing down the track.

Millie broke hard, setting Katie farther back in the saddle. But Katie soon got her balance and urged the mare on. She moved the reins in a scrubbing motion along the filly's neck, encouraging her to head to the front of the pack. By the first-quarter pole, they were setting just off the lead horse's shoulder. Katie looked around, trying to see where the other horses were. This was only a six-furlong race, and already they were flying by the half-mile marker. She stayed low over Millie's withers, listening to the pounding hooves of the horses behind her. She felt the sting of Millie's mane as it whipped across her face. Millie was running easily, her ears pricked in her interest in what lay ahead.

As they rounded the turn, two horses moved up to challenge them. Katie worried that she wouldn't have enough horse left to fend them off. She kept her hold on Millie. She wanted to be sure that her filly had enough in her for the finish line.

As they hit the homestretch, one of the challengers pulled ahead by a nose. Katie heard the wild cheering of the crowd now and the sound of the announcer as he called the race. It was time to move.

She smooched to the filly and cocked her whip into

position. Millie didn't need any more urging. The mare pinned her ears and pulled up beside the lead horse, passing him as she responded to Katie's urging. Katie waved her bat to the side of Millie's face and the filly hung on, fighting to keep her lead.

They crossed the finish line to the deafening roar of the crowd. Katie stood in the irons and looked behind her. They had won by only a head, but they had won!

"Yes!" Katie yelled as she waved her whip in triumph, the way she'd seen other winning jockeys do.

The outrider picked Katie and Millie up on the back turn and escorted them to the winner's circle. Jason flashed her the thumbs-up sign and winked, while her mother bragged about her to anyone who would listen.

Katie couldn't stop smiling as she waited for everyone to get into position for the win photo. By the time they snapped the shot, her face felt ready to break from all the grinning.

"Well, what do you think now?" asked John as Katie jumped down after the last photo and removed the saddle from Millie's back.

Katie stood on the scale for the official weigh-out. "I think I like this racing thing," she said, laughing.

When the man verified that she still carried the correct weight, he waved to the stewards and the race was made official. Katie handed her saddle to the jockey valet and headed for the dressing room. Nancy stood outside the jockeys' quarters waiting for her. She had a funny look on her face.

"What's up, Nancy?" She barely got the words out of

her mouth when Nancy pulled a bucket from behind her back. Katie noticed that the other riders had their own buckets in hand as well. "Oh, no," she laughed, turning to run, but Nancy grabbed her and held her tight.

Katie gasped as the first bucket of mud hit her full in the face. It was followed by several buckets of ice-cold water. She spit and sputtered as the gathering crowd applauded her jockey's initiation.

Nancy then handed her a dry towel. "Congratulations, kid. You're now part of the gang."

⇒ *Chapter Fourteen* ⇒

Katie stood in the middle of the shed row and stared in awe at her new apprentice jockey's license. She hadn't done as well on Ralph Sunday, but they ran through the middle of the pack to finish fourth–and it was a clean ride, so the stewards awarded her a license.

Jason gave Katie a hug that lifted her off the ground. "See, I knew you could do it."

John led Willow King out of the stall and motioned for Jason to leg Katie up. "Now that we've got Katie girl in working order, we've got to get started on this colt. The Santa Anita Derby is only a week away. We can't afford to miss this one if we're going to have a shot in Kentucky."

Katie knotted her reins and placed her feet in the irons. She wanted to be King's jockey in that race so badly, but she knew that she still had very little experience. To make matters worse, she had overheard some of the grooms whispering that plans were being made to use Mark for the race.

The *Daily Racing Form* continued to publish doubting remarks about King's ability to run with the class of horses that were entered in the Derby—especially since they had missed the Jim Beam.

"Who's going to ride King at Santa Anita?" Katie asked, trying to keep her voice casual.

John joined her on the pony-horse. "That's kind of a silly question, isn't it?"

Katie stared at the space between King's ears, ignoring the twinge she felt in her heart. "Yeah. I guess you'd want the most experienced rider up. Mark will be happy that he gets to ride King again. Especially in such a big race."

John looked at her strangely. "Well, he's your horse. You can do what you want with him, but I had assumed that you wanted to ride him."

"I do, John! But do you think it's a good idea? I've only ridden *two* races. The jockeys coming in for the Santa Anita Derby will be the best in the country." Her stomach began to roll at the thought. "I don't think I can compete with that," she said.

"Why not?" asked John.

Katie wondered if the trainer had lost his mind. "Because I don't know anything," she grouched. She wanted so badly to ride King in the big races. But now that she thought about it, she didn't feel she was good enough.

"Even the famous guys make mistakes," John said. "This farm's lost a few races with some big names in the irons. Don't worry yourself none. You'll do just fine."

They had reached the track entrance. John unsnapped the lead rope and Katie backtracked King at a trot.

"Give him two easy miles," John instructed. "We've got to blow some wind back into him."

Although she still felt uneasy about riding King in the

big races, Katie happily cantered her colt around the track. And King went like a champ. It was hard to tell that he had been injured and laid off for almost two weeks. He pulled at the bit and tried to run, but Katie held him to the slower pace. By the time she pulled him up, her arms ached.

Mark visited the shed row each day, asking about King and letting Katie know that he was available to ride in the Santa Anita Derby if she didn't feel up to the challenge.

King's performance over the next several days was good, but the day of his fast work, Katie noticed that something wasn't quite right.

"I don't know, John," Katie said when she pulled King up after a quick breeze and walked him off the track. "He doesn't seem to have the extra *umph* he's had the last few days."

John looked the colt over. "He appears fine, and he's cleaning up all his oats. He's probably just having an off day. We ship him tomorrow, so he'll have a couple days' rest in sunny California. Don't worry, he'll be bright-eyed and ready to go by the time you get there."

Four days later, when Katie stood in the paddock at Santa Anita waiting for a leg up, John's words came back to haunt her. It wasn't anything she could put a finger on, but something was just different about King. He wasn't his usual self. Maybe the travel and days spent in a new barn were hard on him, thought Katie.

John gave Katie the race instructions in the paddock since he wouldn't be ponying her in the post parade as usual. "This is a pretty tough crowd, but there's nothing this horse can't handle," he said as he legged Katie up and walked her out to meet the pony. "Let the speed horses go out front and burn themselves out. You wait somewhere in the center of the pack and make a big push at the end. King likes to run like that."

Katie couldn't help gawking during the post parade. Santa Anita, with its flowers, green lawns, and swaying palm trees, was beautiful. King perked up and strode out as if he was enjoying the scenery too.

They finished the post parade and cantered to the starting gate. Several horses passed them, and Katie smiled to herself when she recognized some of the famous jockeys. She couldn't believe that she was actually there, riding in such incredible company. She said a quick prayer not to goof up.

"Let's load 'em up!" called the starter. The gate was suddenly a hive of activity. The gatemen jumped down from their positions on the starting gate and shouted orders to jockeys and each other.

Katie's helper smiled as he grabbed King's rein. "Don't look so nervous, kid. If you can ride in this kind of company, you'll go far."

Katie returned the smile and prepared herself for the coming race. She pulled her goggles down. The track was dry and in beautiful shape, but Katie knew that goggles were needed in more than just muddy conditions—a rock thrown from the hoof of a running horse could cause a lot of damage.

"Get ready!" the starter called.

Katie stared straight down the track, anticipating the moment the bell would ring. When the gates banged open, she drove King out of the gate, battling for her position.

John was right. The speed horses went directly to the front, setting a blazing pace. Katie held King steady, settling into a good stride in the center of the pack. The race was a mile and three-sixteenths. They had a long way to go.

Katie sat still on King, trying to maintain his pace and keep enough energy for the push down the homestretch. When they had a half-mile left to run, things started happening. The lead horses fell back, and Katie found herself having to steer King around horses that were fading so fast they seemed to be backing up.

"On the inside," a jockey yelled as he drove his horse up beside King.

"Come on, boy," Katie said. She tapped King on the shoulder with her whip, urging him to run with the challenging colt. She felt King gather his strength to go with the other horse.

Katie and King passed several horses going into the final turn. "Come on, King, go for it!" Katie exclaimed. The spray of the sand kicked up from the horses in front of her made tiny clicking noises as it bounced off her goggles. They passed another horse as they came out of the turn and headed down the homestretch. They were in third place and gaining. Her heart thumped with the cadence of King's pounding strides. They could actually win this race.

The jockey next to them pulled his whip and cracked it across his horse's hindquarters, and they surged ahead by a half-length. Katie twirled her bat into place and flagged it in front of King's eyes. She could hear the roar of the crowd as she urged King on, but the momentum he'd had a moment ago faltered. She tagged him on the rump with her whip but got no response.

"Outside," another jockey yelled, pulling alongside them.

King pinned his ears and put up a valiant effort to challenge the gaining horse, but he faded more with each tiring stride. "Come on, boy, we can do it!" Katie pumped the reins back and forth on his neck, but it was a futile effort. King lost more ground, and one more horse passed them at the wire. They finished in fifth place.

Katie stood in the irons and eased King down to a slow gallop, then a trot, before stopping and returning to the finish line to unsaddle.

"I don't know what happened," she told John as she unbuckled the jockey saddle's girth. She wanted to cry but refused to do so in front of all these people. King side-stepped as several horses with their disappointed owners and trainers walked past on their way back to the barn.

Katie pulled her saddle from King's sweaty back and stared at the smiling jockey atop the first-place horse in the winner's circle. "I knew I should have let Mark ride today. He would have known what to do," she said in dismay.

John steadied the blowing horse while one of the valets pulled the race number from his bridle. "There wasn't anything different he could have done. King just lost his steam. He's had two weeks off when all these other horses were racing. He just ran out of gas. Plain and simple. Don't be so hard on yourself, Katie."

Katie handed her saddle to the valet. She saw the flash of the win-photo camera and heard the cheer of the crowd as the race was made official. Losing definitely wasn't as much fun as winning.

John tugged on King's reins and headed toward the

barn. "I'll see you on the back side. The van will be here to get this horse in an hour, and our flight leaves in two. We'll talk on the way home."

Several hours later, Katie saw the lights of Portland come into view from the jet's window. Jason was there to pick them up. He gave Katie a big hug as soon as he saw her. "We watched the race on TV. For a second, I thought you were going to take it all."

Katie felt the lump in her throat rise to choke her. "It's my fault. I should have let Mark ride him," she said, sounding a bit defeated.

John clapped Jason on the shoulder and handed him his travel bag. "I keep trying to tell this hardheaded girl that there was nothing she could have done any differently. But she won't listen."

Jason pulled Katie's travel bag from her shoulder and hefted it onto his own. "I think John's right, Kat. I watched the replay several times, and you were never bumped or boxed in. King just didn't have it today. He had a long time off waiting for his shoulder to heal. We were asking a lot of him to run in that Grade 1 stakes race."

Katie shrugged her shoulders. She wasn't convinced. "There must have been something I could have done."

Jason laughed. "Outside of getting off and carrying him, I don't know what."

Katie smiled for the first time since the race. "What time does King get in?"

John looked at his watch. "It takes the van about sixteen hours to make that run from Los Angeles. He'll be there when you get up tomorrow morning."

"I think I'll get up early and be there when the van pulls in," Katie said as she pushed the airport terminal door open and stepped into the cool evening air.

As she followed Jason to the truck, Katie couldn't shake the feeling that she had done something wrong during the race. She took a deep breath and stared at the stars overhead. *Mark would have known what to do,* she thought. Then she frowned. She was sure Mark would tell her all about her mistakes when she saw him tomorrow.

Katie thanked Jason for the ride when he dropped her off at her house. Then she trudged up the front steps, feeling very tired. She spent some time rehashing the race with her mother, but soon she excused herself and went up to bed. It had been a very long day.

She slept only a few hours, tossing and turning as she dreamed about the race. She finally gave up on the idea of getting a good night's rest and got up in the wee hours of the morning to go to Willow Run and wait for the horse van.

She sat in a chair in the tack room, wrapped in a horse blanket, and drifted back to sleep. She woke when she heard the van rumble into the stable yard.

Katie tossed the blanket aside and rose from the chair. She was stiff from sleeping in a cramped position. The large truck braked in front of the barn, and she went out to greet the driver. He handed her papers to sign, then went to fetch King.

Katie heard the sound of hoofbeats on wood as King walked down the exit ramp. Her heart gave a small lurch at the sight of him. Something wasn't right.

"You better call the vet," said the driver, handing King's

lead rope to Katie. "He doesn't look very good. It could be shipping fever."

Katie led King to his stall. He moved with his head low-ered, dragging his feet. She felt his ears to see if they were warm, indicating that he might have a fever. They were hot to the touch.

King walked into his freshly made stall and inspected his feed bucket. Katie held her breath, hoping he would take a mouthful of the oats, but he only blew softly through his lips and turned away, standing with his head down in the clean straw. She ran to John's small house on the edge of Willow Run's property. She banged on the door until the porch light came on.

"What's wrong?" John said, rubbing the sleep from his eyes.

"King's in trouble. We need to call the vet," Katie said as she wrung her hands. "The driver thought he might have shipping fever. He doesn't look good at all." Katie brushed her hair from her wild eyes.

"Now don't go thinking that way, Katie girl," John warned. "You get back to the colt. I'll be down with the vet."

By the time Katie reached his stall, King was coughing, and she noticed a small amount of mucus running out of his nose. His sides heaved as he tried to draw in a deep breath. "Easy, fella," she crooned as she slipped a light blanket onto his back. "The vet will be here soon."

Twenty minutes later, Dr. Marvin and John pulled up to the barn. Katie ran out to meet them. "He's getting worse. He won't eat or drink anything. I've got him blanketed." She led the way back to the stall.

"Let's see what we've got here." Dr. Marvin pulled out

his thermometer to take King's temperature. He listened to the colt's heart and lungs while he waited for the temperature reading to be complete.

Katie held King's lead rope while the vet ran his hands over the horse's body, poking and prodding here and there.

"Ahhh," the doctor said as he palpated something under King's jawbone. The thermometer beeped and he checked the reading. "Hmm. He's running a fever of a hundred and three degrees. That's not good. It'll probably go higher before he's through this."

Katie exhaled deeply. "Is it shipping fever?"

The vet shook his head. "No. Come here and feel this." He guided Katie's hand to the large cystlike bumps under King's jawbone. "Looks like he's got a case of the strangles."

"Strangles?" Katie was shocked. "But he's had his strangles shot. How could this happen?"

John replaced the blanket that the vet had removed. "Just because he's had the shot doesn't mean he *can't* get sick. It means that if he does, he won't get it as bad as he would if he didn't have the shot."

Katie stared at her sick horse. It was hard to imagine that he could have it worse. "Can he die?"

The vet looked in the eye sympathetically. "That's a possibility. But if we keep on top of this thing, he'll come out okay. I'll come by tomorrow and lance those knots under his throat. They're full of infection. You need to make sure that you keep his dirty bedding and buckets away from the other horses. He's already exposed them by being here, so there's no sense moving him."

"What about a shot?" Katie said. "Is there penicillin or something you can give him?"

Dr. Marvin shook his head. "That would only drive the infection inward, and that could kill him. No, we've got to wait until those pockets fill up. Then we'll lance them and get rid of the bad stuff."

"We're in for a long haul, Katie," John said. "King will be sick for several days. And you don't look so good yourself. Why don't you go home—I'll take over from here."

"No. He's my horse. I've seen him through everything else. I'm staying." Katie grabbed her blanket, and John helped her pull a bale of straw over in front of Willow King's stall. "Could you please call my mom and tell her I'll be staying at the barn for a while."

She sat on the bale and wrapped the blanket around her body, listening to her horse wheeze as he drew each breath. "It'll be okay, ol' buddy. We've gone through so much together. I'm not losing you now."

⇒ *Chapter Fifteen* ⇒

Katie heard the tapping of Camela's cane as she made her way up the shed row. The young girl's face was full of concern.

"Katie?" Camela called. "Katie, are you still here?"

"I'm over here, next to King," Katie said as she shifted in her chair. She had been sitting for hours, listening to King's ragged breathing, and her legs were falling asleep. She wished there were something she could do to keep busy. But the only thing she could do for King was to stay where she was and give him comfort.

Camela stopped in front of Katie's chair. "I heard that King wasn't feeling well," she said. "Is he really sick?"

"Yeah, he's pretty bad," Katie said, rising and going to the tack room to get another folding chair for Camela.

Camela sat quietly for several moments, fidgeting with the end of her cane. "Is King going to die?" she whispered, her voice cracking with each painful word.

Katie stood and leaned on King's door, watching over the big horse as he lay in the deep straw, his breathing raspy and uneven. "Dr. Marvin said it's a possibility, but I don't think it's going to happen," she said, trying to sound braver than she felt. "King's a strong horse. He'll pull out of this."

A tear trickled down Camela's cheek. "It's all my fault," she said in utter misery. "If I hadn't forgotten to check King's door latch, he wouldn't have gotten out and eaten where the sick horses eat."

Katie went to Camela and hugged her. "It's not your fault, Cam. We don't even know what caused King's sickness. This could be a virus he picked up in Southern California. It might not have anything to do with him getting out of his stall last week."

Camela ran the sleeve of her shirt across her face. "But it *could* have been my fault," she asserted. "I feel so bad that your horse might be sick because of me." Camela reached for Katie's arm. "I want to help, Katie. Please don't say I can't."

Katie smiled at her friend. "Dr. Marvin says there's not much we can do for King right now. But I'd be glad to have your company if you don't mind sitting here."

Katie pushed a strand of her tangled hair behind her ear and looked around the deserted stable. It was Sunday, and most of the staff had the day off. "It's been really quiet at the barn today," she said. "I really thought Mark would be here to tell me what a rotten race I rode." Katie sank farther into her chair, her mind going over the race for the hundredth time.

"It wasn't your fault that King ran fifth," Camela said. "Maybe he didn't have the energy because he was starting to get sick."

Katie thought about that for a moment. Camela might be right. It was very unusual that King didn't have the energy to make the big push down the stretch to the finish line.

Katie chuckled. "Well, at least I can use that excuse when Mark lectures me for placing so poorly."

"Mark's in Kentucky," Camela said.

"Kentucky?" Katie sat straight up in her chair. "What is Mark doing in Kentucky?"

Camela shrugged her shoulders. "I don't know for sure, but I heard him talking to Cindy, and it sounds like he might have a horse to ride in the Derby. He left last night to go ride for the trainer. It's somebody he used to race for in New York."

Katie bit her lip. She wasn't sure how she felt about this. One part of her was glad that Mark was going to get his wish to ride in the Kentucky Derby—even if it wasn't on Willow King. But the other part of her worried that they wouldn't have Mark to fall back on if something happened and Katie couldn't ride.

King stirred in his stall, rising unsteadily to his feet. He coughed deeply and wheezed several times. Katie unlatched the door and went to him, laying a comforting hand on his fevered coat. She hated feeling helpless, and she hated seeing King so sick. But Dr. Marvin had said that it would be several days before they saw an improvement. There was nothing she could do but wait.

The next several days passed in a blur as Katie spent morning, noon, and night at King's side. Her mother brought her meals and even sat with King on several occasions after she forced Katie to go home and shower or rest in her own bed.

Jason came down during the evenings, sleeping on an old cot in the tack room to make sure Katie was safe.

Camela came and went, sitting silently by Katie's side. Katie knew that Camela blamed herself for King's being sick, and nothing Katie said could convince her otherwise.

Luckily for Katie, it was spring break, so she could stay at the barn for as long as she wanted to during the day. They were now less than four weeks away from the Kentucky Derby, and with every ragged breath King took, her hopes of seeing the big colt prove himself in the Derby slipped farther and farther away.

Katie rose to check on King again. The big bay colt lay stretched out in his stall, refusing to eat or drink. Each ragged breath he drew pained Katie to the bone.

King stirred on the straw, lifting his head to look at Katie before groaning and lying back against the thick bedding. If King would just drink something, he might be able to break the fever. At the least, it would help rehydrate his body.

Katie knelt beside King, running a cool sponge behind his ears and over his poll.

"How's he doing?" Camela's head poked over the door.

Katie jumped. "I didn't hear you come up the shed row." She ran another spongeful of water over King's coat. "Dr. Marvin said that if King isn't any better by tomorrow morning, he's going to run an IV tube to pump some liquids into him."

"Can't we force him to drink?" Camela asked.

Katie smiled for the first time in days. "You know the old saying, *'You can lead a horse to water, but you can't make him drink'?*" Camela's brow furrowed. "But what about that drench gun you were telling me they used to wash the horse's mouth out before a race?" she asked.

Katie paused. Then a big smile formed on her lips.

"Camela, you're a genius!" She laid the sponge aside and ran to the tack room. She threw open the cabinet door and tore through the contents that lined the shelves. When she didn't find what she was looking for, she turned the tack box upside down. Her eyes lit on the drench gun. She snatched it from the floor and hurriedly filled a gallon can with cool water and liquid vitamins.

"I want to help," Camela insisted.

Katie grabbed her hand, guiding the young girl into King's stall. She could feel Camela's hand shake and knew how hard this must be for her. Camela still hadn't lost her fear of horses.

When they entered the stall, King rolled his eyes in their direction and took a labored breath, coughing when he inhaled too deeply.

"Easy, boy. I've got something I want to try." Katie eased down beside King and lifted his head into her lap.

Camela filled the drench gun with the water-and vitamin mixture and handed it to Katie.

King tried to resist when Katie inserted the gun into the side of his mouth, but he relaxed as she slowly squeezed the water onto the back of his tongue.

At first the water rolled out the side of King's mouth, spilling onto Katie's jeans. She tried another syringe, and this time King licked his lips. "That's it, boy. Let's try it again. There's plenty more where this came from."

"Is it working?" Camela asked excitedly. "Is he drinking?"

"I think it's going to work," Katie said as she inserted another load of water and King responded by sucking the wetness off his tongue. Katie wanted to leap up and shout, but that would have to wait until later. They weren't out of the woods yet. "Can you get some more water, Camela?" Katie asked, placing the empty can into the girl's hand.

Camela nodded vigorously and made her way out of the stall and down the shed row to the water spigot.

Katie and Camela managed to get several more cans of the lifesaving liquid down King's throat. By morning, he was standing on shaky legs and drinking on his own.

"I don't know what you did," Dr. Marvin said when he examined King later that morning. "But I think we're finally over the hump. Another couple days and he'll be hollering for his breakfast, and a week after that, he'll be ready to go back into training."

"And not a minute too soon," John said. "By then, we'll only have two and a half weeks until the Kentucky Derby."

Katie breathed a huge sigh of relief. It was good to hear talk of the Derby again. It meant things were going to be all right.

True to Dr. Marvin's prediction, King was back in action within a week after his fever broke. He had lost a lot of conditioning, but he was coming back and training strong.

One day after school, when Katie arrived at her regular gallop time, Jason met her at the head of the shed row with a big smile on his face.

"You're awfully cheerful this evening," she said. "What's up?"

Jason took off his hat and flapped it against his leg. "John entered Willow King for Saturday's race card."

"*This* Saturday?" Katie stopped in her tracks. "I thought John decided to skip that race. Saturday's only a couple of days away. How's he going to get King shipped all the way back east and settled in that soon?"

"No, silly." Jason reached out and tweaked one of Katie's braids. "King is going to run here at Portland Downs. He's training like a champ, so John's decided to pass up one of the big races back east in order to keep him close to home a little longer. We ship to Kentucky five days after this race."

"Who did he name as rider?" Katie asked tentatively. She had done so poorly on King last time, she wouldn't blame John for putting a more experienced rider up.

"Kat, you've got to stop beating yourself up over that last race," Jason said as he put an arm around her shoulder and led her to the tack room. "You can't win them all. You've been doing fine as King's jockey."

"You really think so?" she asked. Jason's opinion had always meant a lot to her. And she knew that Jason would never lie.

"I think you've got a great career ahead of you," he said as he plopped his hat back on his head. "Even though I do hold my breath every time I watch you ride. I don't like it when some of those other jockeys cause trouble."

Katie laughed. "As long as I've got you here to pick up the pieces, I'll be okay."

Jason's smile faded and he grew serious. "Don't joke about that, Kat. You know that accidents happen all the time in this business. I don't want to see you get hurt."

Katie took Jason's hand, giving it a reassuring squeeze. "I'm always careful. Don't worry about me."

Jason grabbed the tack and headed out of the tack room. "Oh, I almost forgot," he said, glancing back over his shoulder. "Mark's coming back for the stakes race we've got King entered in on Saturday. So you'll be riding against your teacher."

Katie opened her mouth several times to speak, but no words came out. She felt like a fish out of water. She was going to ride against Mark! Her stomach did a flip-flop just thinking about it.

Jason threw the saddle on a bale of straw and leaned on King's stall door. "From what John said, Mark's drawn a horse for the Derby, but he's hinting to John that he'd pull off that horse to ride King." Jason rubbed King's head as the big bay stepped to the front of his stall. "Katie, I know you've got a lot of faith in Mark, and he's done a good job teaching you, but I still don't trust the guy. I think you really need to watch him in this race. I think he's going to try to show you up."

Katie took a deep breath. She knew how badly Mark wanted to ride King in the Kentucky Derby, but he was supposed to be her friend. Would he cause trouble just to get her mount?

Katie didn't have a lot of time for debate. With King's upcoming race on Saturday, and the Kentucky Derby only two weeks away, she had plenty to keep her busy.

She looked forward to Saturday's race with excitement—and a bit of dread. She couldn't wait to race King again, but she was a little intimidated about riding against Mark.

When Saturday finally arrived, Katie was more nervous than ever. Her mother had made her favorite breakfast of waffles with fresh strawberries, but Katie hadn't been able to eat more than two bites.

They loaded their car and picked up Jan, then made the

hour drive to Portland. Jason and John had left with King early that morning so that the big colt would have a few hours to settle in before race time.

"Here we are," Mrs. Durham said as she turned into the gates of Portland Downs.

Katie's heart sped up when she saw the tall pines that lined the outside curve of the track at the clubhouse turn. Just a few more hours and she'd be riding King in a stakes race!

After a quick stop on the back side to see how King was doing, Katie headed to the front side of the track where the jockeys' quarters were located. King didn't run until the seventh race, but Katie wanted to get to the jockeys' room early to make sure all her equipment was ready and in good repair.

Katie could hear the announcer call the races from inside the jockeys' quarters. She did a quick check of her equipment and looked around for Nancy. When she couldn't find her, she slipped out to watch a few races from the jockeys' private, fenced-in area. She had only been there five minutes when she heard a familiar voice.

"Katie, how you doing?" Mark said as he came to stand beside her on the fence. "I guess we're racing against each other today, huh?" He thumbed through his program and pointed out both their names on the racing card. "Looks like King's one of the favorites," he said.

Katie nodded and smiled.

"Are you nervous?" he asked, brushing his blond hair off his forehead and giving her a big grin.

Katie nodded. "Do you ever get over the nervous part?"

Mark rubbed his chin and looked at the horses getting

ready to load into the starting gate. "It gets easier," he said. "But I still get edgy when I've got a big race to ride."

They sat in silence for a moment. Then Mark spoke again. "So you still think you want to ride King in the Derby?"

Katie's stomach rolled. If she was this nervous for a small-stakes race on her home turf, how bad was she going to be at the Kentucky Derby?

Mark turned to face Katie, his look growing serious. "I still think you should reconsider letting me ride King for you, Katie. In a race like the Derby, you'll be going against the best riders in the country. There's a million-dollar purse at stake, and you're going to want the best shot you've got."

Katie just stared at him. Was he implying that she wasn't good enough? Mark must have seen the irritation on her face, because he was quick to explain his words.

"Now, don't get me wrong," he said as he put a hand on her shoulder. "You're a fine rider. You're one of my best students. But let's face it, both of us know that you don't have much experience. You know I'd give King my very best if I rode him in the Derby."

"But you already have a mount," Katie said. She turned, preparing to leave. Their conversation was making her uncomfortable.

Mark moved around to block her exit. "Yes, I do. But he's not half the horse that King is. Despite what the *Racing Form* says, I think King has a shot at winning the Derby if he has the right rider up. I'd pull off that other mount if you gave me a shot at King."

Katie stared into Mark's blue eyes, seeing his confidence. "And you think you're the best jockey for Willow

192

King?"

"Of course I do," he laughed, smacking his whip smartly against his boots. "I think you know it too, Katie." He put his arm around her shoulders and steered her back to the jockeys' quarters. "You've ridden several races. You know what kind of trouble a horse can get into out there. King needs an experienced jockey who can keep him out of the jams and get him across the finish line first." Mark stopped and thumped his chest. "That's me."

Katie stared at Mark, expecting to see his head swell as they stood there. She had always known he had an ego, but not just how big it was. She took a deep breath and let it out slowly. Mark was right about the experience part, but *she* knew King the best. He would run better for her.

"Well, you think about it, Katie. We've got two weeks until the Derby," he said as he reached out to shake her hand. "Good luck in today's race. I hope one of us makes it to the winner's circle."

Katie watched Mark walk boldly into the jockeys' room, feeling her confidence ebb with every step he took. Had she made the right decision? Was she the best choice for Willow King in the Derby?

An hour later, as she sat in the starting gate waiting for the rest of the horses to be loaded in, Katie steeled her resolve and vowed to beat Mark in this race. She'd show him that she could ride as well as he could.

King had drawn the number-three position. Mark was two stalls over in the five hole. He looked over at Katie and smiled. Katie didn't smile back.

John's instructions to her were the same as they'd been at Santa Anita: *Stay in the middle of the pack, and make a run for it at the end.* Katie pulled her goggles down and waited for the starter's command.

"Get tied on!"

She grabbed a handful of mane and glanced over at Mark. He was staring right at her.

"See you at the finish line, Katie," he yelled over the snorts of the anxious horses.

The bell rang and Katie sent King out of the gate, jockeying for a position along the rail. When King settled into his stride, she looked to see where Mark and his mount were.

Mark was positioned in the back of the pack, running in the middle of the track. Katie breathed easier and got her mind back to the race. They were only going a mile, and they were quickly approaching the half-mile marker. Katie asked King for a little more run, and he moved up along the rail, passing a couple of horses. It felt great to have a healthy horse under her again. She could feel that King had plenty to give.

They moved into the turn and passed another horse. Katie could see the hindquarters of the three horses running side by side in front of her. She would have to go wide out of the turn and pass them on the outside. And she knew that she had plenty of horse left to do it.

As they rounded the turn, she glanced over her shoulder to make sure the way was clear before swinging to the outside.

"Looking for somewhere to go?" Mark said as he pulled his horse alongside Willow King, effectively closing off the path.

"Get out of the way, Mark!" Katie shouted over the roar of the crowd. The sand kicked up from the horses in front of her was pelting her face and sticking to her teeth.

"I can't do that, Katie," Mark hollered over the pounding hooves as he pulled his whip and cracked his horse across the hindquarters. "I want to win, and you've got more horse than me. If I let you out, you'll pass us and win. An experienced rider would have known better than to ride King into that hole. Racing strategy comes with *experience*," he shouted arrogantly.

They were down to the eighth pole. Katie thought about pulling up and going all the way around Mark, but there wasn't enough time. She couldn't squeeze through and bump him either or she'd be disqualified for interference.

The sound of the crowd reverberated in her ears as her mind reeled, searching for a way out of this trap. Mark went to work on his horse, and the colt surged ahead, clearing the way for Katie to pull out and around the fading leaders. But it was too late. She saw the flash of the photo-finish camera as Mark crossed the line a length ahead of her.

Katie was practically in tears by the time she got King pulled up and returned to the unsaddling area. Mark tipped his whip to her from the winner's circle as she pulled the saddle from King's back. She ignored him and went to the scales for her weigh-in.

While she waited for the official to clear her, an obnoxious little man with a fat cigar stood on the other side of the fence tearing up his tickets. He threw them in her face.

"Go back to your knitting needles, little girl. You sure don't know how to ride racehorses. I lost fifty bucks on you!" said the little man.

Katie gasped as the sharp edges of the tickets bounced off her cheek. How could anyone be so cruel? When the official waved her on, Katie tossed her saddle to the valet and ran to the jockeys' room. She just wanted to get away from here. The man was right. Her inexperience had caused King to lose. And maybe Mark was right—maybe he was the best choice for King in the Derby.

~ *Chapter Sixteen* ~

"I'm *not* riding in the Kentucky Derby!" Katie screamed at Jason as she paced up and down the shed row. "I can't even win a lousy race at home. How can you expect me to ride in the most famous race in the world when I can't even win a small-stakes race here? Mark was right. I'm not experienced enough to ride King in the Derby." Katie plopped herself down on a bale of straw and stubbornly crossed her arms, daring Jason to argue with her.

Jason ran a hand through his hair, then shook his head in exasperation. "So that's it? You're just going to give up and let Mark ride King in the Derby?"

"Yup," Katie said as she nodded. "That just about sums it up."

Jason threw his hands in the air and stomped down the shed row. "John, would you get over here and talk some sense into this girl?" he said to the trainer.

John put down his copy of the *Daily Racing Form* and joined the conversation. "I already tried. This gal's head is so thick that nothing can get in."

Katie frowned at both of them. "I'm doing what's best

for my horse. Why can't you guys understand that?"

Jason hunkered down on his heels in front of Katie. "Because we think the best thing for King is that *you* ride him. He trusts you, Katie. He'll run for you like nobody else. You would have won that race by a mile if you hadn't gotten boxed in."

Now it was Katie's turn to be aggravated. "That's just it!" she shouted. "I *did* get him boxed in. *I* lost the race for him! Can't you see that?"

Jason rolled his eyes skyward as if he were talking to a stubborn child. "So are you planning to give up riding altogether?"

Katie stood and busied her hands by straightening the tack. They weren't going to let up. "No, I just think it would be better if I rode a few more small races around here before I jump into the big time." She took a deep breath and exhaled slowly. "I never realized how much damage a small mistake could cause. We can't afford that kind of a mistake in the Derby."

John pulled the hay net from Willow King's stall and loaded it with several flakes of grass hay. "Everyone makes mistakes. That's how you learn."

Katie grabbed the next empty hay net, handing it to John. "That's true. But in the Kentucky Derby, a mistake could cost you first place. Or worse yet, somebody's life."

"But, Katie," Jason said, "that's the nature of the business. You're either a jockey and you deal with it, or you can't stand the heat and you get out. You're going to have to make up your mind."

"I *do* plan to ride," Katie said. "Just not in the Derby. Mark is the best jockey for King in that race." She looked into Jason's eyes, pleading with him to understand. He knew how badly she wanted to ride King at Churchill Downs, but she really thought it would be better for King if she didn't.

"What about Millie?" John finished filling the hay nets and took Katie's vacated seat on the straw bale. "I was planning to ship her back to Kentucky with King so he'd feel more at home. There's a nice race for her on Derby day. It's a small allowance race. Could you handle that?"

Katie perked up. An allowance race. That would give her the opportunity to ride at Churchill Downs without the burden of botching up a major race. She bit her tongue to keep the smile from reaching her lips. She didn't want to seem too anxious after throwing a fit about riding King. But the truth was, she'd give up just about anything to be able to ride at *that* track on *that* day. "Sure. I could do that," she said.

John slapped her on the back and smiled. "Good, then it's all settled. I'll make the travel arrangements. Jason and I will share a room, and we'll get one for you, Jan, and your mom. We'll need to get you there a couple days early so you can get licensed and get a feel for the track." He stood and stretched his back. "We've got a lot to get done before we leave. I expect some hard work out of both of you in the next few days because we've got some races to win!"

Katie spent the next few days in a panic, trying to get the horses ready to ship and herself packed. She was going to miss a couple of days of school, so she had to get advance assignments and turn them in before she left.

It was a relief when they finally boarded the plane to

Kentucky. Jan was excited and wanted to talk, but Katie was so tired that she couldn't keep her eyes open. She fell asleep to the sound of her mother and her best friend discussing the new hats and dresses they had purchased for the great day. Katie smiled. Bonnets on Derby day were a sight to behold, and the more flamboyant, the better. Jan would fit right in with her bright purple feathered hat.

Katie slept for most of the flight, waking only when Jason shook her to point out the airport below. After a smooth landing, they gathered their bags, rented a car, and were soon on their way to the racetrack.

Churchill Downs! Katie could hardly believe she was in Louisville, Kentucky, heading for one of the most famous racetracks in the United States. The airport was only two miles from the track, so it wasn't long before the twin white spires of Churchill Downs' grandstands came into view.

Katie's breath caught in her throat. She had seen this view on television many times, but it couldn't compare with the real thing. As they skirted the track, heading for the back side, Katie caught glimpses of the dirt and turf courses, the beautiful red tulips, and the huge tote board where the horses' odds were posted. She knew the Kentucky Derby Museum was on the front side, as well as some famous life-sized horse statues. She couldn't wait to go see them.

"Wow!" Katie said when they pulled into the parking lot on the horsemen's side of the track.

Jason got out of the car and held the door open for them. "It's a little bigger than we're used to," he said, laughing.

Mrs. Durham stepped from the car. "I was reading some information about Churchill Downs. Do you know they have forty-eight barns here, *plus* a receiving barn, detention barn, *and* pony barn?"

Katie couldn't keep the smile off her face. She'd only been here a few minutes and she already loved it.

"Don't forget, our home is in *Oregon*," Jan joked as she grabbed Katie by the arm and dragged her toward the entrance gate.

John locked the car, and they went to see if King and Millie had arrived. The guard at the gate consulted his clipboard and nodded.

"Your horses arrived an hour ago. You can find them in stalls ten and eleven in the receiving barn." He motioned them through the gate.

As they walked to the receiving barn, Jason winked at Katie. "Feels good to be here, doesn't it?"

Katie glanced around, her excitement building as she took in all the activity. It was midafternoon, and the grooms were scurrying about doing their daily routines of feeding and cleaning stalls. Some horses were out on the hotwalker, while others stood in their stalls whinnying for their rations.

Several of the large training barns had their shed rows decorated in stable colors, and flowering plants and shrubs lined their walkways. Katie wondered which of these magnificent Thoroughbreds would be running against King in the Derby.

When they turned the corner, Katie heard a familiar whinny and went immediately to Willow King's stall. "Hey, boy, how'd you like flying in that jet?" She held King's halter while John and Jason checked to make sure he had-n't been injured during the trip. Both Millie and King checked out well.

They spent almost an hour getting the horses settled. Then they went to check in at their hotel. Mark was staying at the same place. His room was just down the hall. Katie felt a jealous pang every time she looked at him. If only she'd had enough experience under her belt. Then she would have let herself ride King in the Derby!

Katie could hardly sleep that night with all the thoughts racing around in her head. The next several days were going to be some of the most exciting days of her life—even if she wasn't riding King.

The following morning, as Katie stepped Millie off the track from their morning workout, she saw the press gathered around Mark and Willow King. The thrill of having just completed her first gallop on the famous Kentucky Derby track dulled as she watched Mark smile and answer questions while posing for the cameras.

King was the longest shot in this race, but the press loved a good story, and King had come a long way from that crooked-legged foal she had saved three years ago. A great rush of pride pushed aside her jealousy. King was a remarkable horse. He had already beaten the odds just by being here.

She turned Millie away from the hoopla and headed back to the barn, telling herself it didn't matter that she could have been riding King. Mark was a good jockey, and he deserved the publicity. She'd get her small measure of fame tomorrow when she rode Millie in the fourth race. Of course, she'd be the only one who knew it was a *famous* moment, but that didn't matter. It would be *her* moment. Now was the time for Mark and King.

She handed Millie over to a groom that John had hired and waited for Mark and King at the barn. She caught King as Mark dismounted and ran to catch another horse he had picked up for the sixth race on Derby day.

Katie bathed King, then put him on the hotwalker to cool out. While she was cleaning his stall, another batch of media personnel tromped down the aisle. She ducked into the tack room and let John handle the interview. They sure were giving a lot of attention to a horse that was expected to run way back in the field of sixteen entries.

Of course, Katie knew that King was capable of winning the Derby, but the experts didn't care about her opinion.

John opened the door to the tack room. "It's all clear. Who would have thought you'd be camera-shy?"

Katie lowered her eyes and kicked at a dust bunny that crawled across the floor. "I'm not shy. I just didn't want to get in the way. It was your moment. You deserved all the attention." John gave her his you-don't-fool-me look, so Katie changed the subject. "I'm ready to go back to the hotel. Is King finished?"

John picked up the lead rope. "Let me put him away and we'll be all set. We've got a busy day tomorrow. We better get all the rest we can."

Rest? How can I get any rest? thought Katie. Tomorrow she would be riding on the most famous track in the country, and her horse would be running in the Kentucky Derby! Sleep was not an option—it was an impossibility!

*　　*　　*

Derby day dawned with a cloud-covered sky. There were so many things to do that the morning passed in a flash. Before she knew it, Katie was standing in the jockeys' room, staring at the hundreds of racing silks hanging on the wall.

In Oregon, the jockeys' silks were owned by the state, and you wore the color that was assigned to the starting position your horse drew. In Kentucky, all the horse owners had their own silks.

Katie smiled as she stared at the rainbow of colors that draped the wall. She spotted the blue-and-white silks of Willow Run Farm. Soon she would be putting them on for Millie's race. Then Mark would get to wear them for the Derby.

Katie changed into her jockey pants and boots and went to do her official weigh-in. By the time she finished checking her goggles and saddle and grabbed the blue-and-white silks off the wall, they were calling the riders for the fourth race.

Katie stepped out of the jockeys' quarters, awed at the large number of people crowded around the paddock. She had heard the announcer say that there were over a hundred thousand people in the stands and infield for this year's Run for the Roses.

She waved to her mother and Jan, then scanned the crowd, looking for Camela and the Ellis family. They were supposed to have arrived this morning. Tom Ellis saw Katie first and waved to her from their spot at the rear of the paddock viewing area.

The buzz of the crowd hummed in Katie's ears as she forced herself to quit gawking and make her way to Millie's saddling stall. Old John gave her the instructions, and Jason gave her a leg her up. "Smile, Kat. You can do this," Jason said encouragingly.

Katie sat up straighter. Jason was right. She *could* do this. The bugle called them to the post, and the pony led them through the post parade.

Katie stared out over the crowd. There were people everywhere, both in the stands and on the infield. Everyone smiled as they waved their programs and raised their mint juleps in toasts to this exciting event. She was amazed that so many people would show up when rain was predicted for the day.

Katie couldn't keep the smile off her face. She was here. *She was actually here.* Even though she wouldn't be riding King, this was still a dream come true. She kicked Millie into a canter as they headed back to the starting gate.

"Good luck," her pony-person called as she turned Katie over to the gateman.

"Thanks." Katie smiled as she pulled her goggles down and helped the gateman guide Millie into the three hole. John's instruction had been simple: *"This filly's got plenty of speed. It's a six-furlong race. Get her out on the engine and go wire-to-wire."*

Katie felt a drop of rain touch her face. She raised her palm to the air. Several more drops hit her hand. She hoped the rain would hold off until after King's race.

The horses stomped nervously in the gate, ready to be off. Katie patted Millie, speaking softly to her as she looked out of the gate at the perfectly harrowed racecourse. The track was listed as *fast* at the moment, but that could change quickly if the rain came.

"Two more horses to load and we're all in!" somebody

yelled from behind the gate.

Katie readied Millie. They had to get out fast and get a good position on the rail. The *Daily Racing Form* had them picked to run eighth out of twelve entries. The *Form* didn't seem to like horses from Oregon very well. They might just be in for a big surprise today, Katie thought.

"All in and ready to go!" the gateman called.

Katie held on tight, tuning all her senses for the moment when the doors would spring open. The bell sounded and she smooched Millie out of the gate, asking her for a burst of speed that would propel them to the front of the crowd. The filly responded, lengthening her stride and driving to the front of the herd.

Katie picked her spot on the rail and sat tight, letting Millie run at her own pace. They were alone in the front, but Katie knew that wouldn't last long. They were already approaching the final turn, and she could feel somebody moving up on the outside. She held her filly steady, waiting for the homestretch before making her move.

When they rounded the turn, Katie pulled her whip and flagged it to the side of Millie's face. The filly drove forward, ears pinned, but the red horse next to them matched her stride for stride.

Katie popped Millie once, then went to hand-riding her, scrubbing the reins along the filly's neck in an attempt to push her faster.

The roar of the crowd was deafening as they approached the finish line. Katie had never heard a hundred thousand people screaming at once. It was exhilarating! She glanced at the jockey next to her. He was down flat on his horse's back, asking his mount for everything it had.

He wanted to win this race as badly as she did.

The red horse stuck to them like glue. Katie popped Millie again and smooched in the filly's ears. "Come on, Millie, run!" With only a few lengths to the finish wire, Katie knew it might be a dead heat. But she didn't want a tie. She wanted to win. She flagged Millie with the whip again and remembered the trick Mark had taught her.

At the wire, Katie stuck her whip under Millie's chin and tapped her, causing the filly to raise her head slightly. The camera flashed, and Katie stood in the irons, praying that her tactic had worked.

Katie gradually slowed her mount, then returned to the unsaddling area. The sign was posted for a photo finish. She circled her horse with the other jockey, waiting for the stewards to make a decision.

The roar of the crowd alerted Katie that the winner had been posted on the tote board. She turned to look and let out a whoop when she saw that Millie had won.

John grabbed the filly's reins and steered them to the winner's circle. "That was a great move, tipping Millie's nose up at the finish line. You won by a whisker!"

Katie could hardly contain herself as she circled Millie, waiting for her friends and family to make it into the winner's circle. She had won a race at Churchill Downs!

A flash of movement by the jockeys' quarters caught Katie's eye, and she turned to see Mark standing on the fence with his thumb up. He motioned with his whip to tell her he was proud of her for using his trick.

"All right, let's get the horse into position," the track photographer called. "Everyone ready?"

Katie smiled for the photo, then weighed out and ran to

the jockeys' room to clean up. Mark would be riding his other mount in the next race coming up. Then two races after that was the Kentucky Derby! She hurried off to make sure she'd be ready to watch King in the big race.

Katie cleaned up in record time. She had just shut off her hair dryer when she heard the sound of a siren approaching. She heard feet running and peeked out the door to see what was happening. "What's going on?" she asked a young jockey who was just returning from the sixth race.

The kid pulled off his helmet and swiped his sleeve across his wet face. "This rain is making the track slick. Two riders went down, and they're taking them to the hospital now. One was scheduled to ride in the Derby." He wiped his face again and turned to enter the men's quarters.

Katie ignored the drizzling rain and stepped onto the deck. The medics were loading a stretcher into the ambulance. She gasped when she saw who was on it.

Mark had been in the accident!

⇒ *Chapter Seventeen* ⇒

"Katie!" someone called from the other side of the fence.

Katie snapped her head around to see Cindy, Jan, and Camela standing on the other side of the paddock. She hurried to the fence.

"Mark is hurt. You've got to ride King," Camela blurted out, her fingers clenching the cyclone fence as she pressed her face against the thick wire.

"Are you sure it was him?" Katie asked, even though she knew the answer before asking the question—she had seen his face, before Mark was loaded into the ambulance. "I just don't know," Katie said, shaking her head and looking at the crowd of umbrellas on the infield. "There are so many great jockeys here. There's got to be someone who can ride King." She ignored the crushed look that came over Camela's face.

Cindy waved John and Jason over to the fence. "She doesn't want to ride King. She says we can find a better jockey, but I think she's just plain *chicken.*" Cindy put her hands on her hips and glared at Katie. Katie wanted to throttle the little fink.

John pushed his way to the front. "Your mother's upstairs with Tom Ellis. She said she'd support any decision you make, but I think she'd like to see you ride as much as the rest of us would." With that said, the old trainer patiently waited for an answer.

Katie stared at the faces before her. They just didn't understand. She held her ground. "I think Mark was right when he said that Willow King needed an experienced rider for this race."

Camela stomped her foot and frowned heavily. "*Mark* wanted to ride Willow King. He wasn't speaking of any other *experienced rider* but himself. Remember, you told me we had all our haystacks tied down, Katie. You've got nothing to fear." She crossed her arms and pouted. "Didn't you always tell me to believe in myself? Well, why should I if you don't?"

Katie saw the tear that slipped down her friend's cheek and felt her insides twist. Should she ride and let King down? Or should she chicken out and let Camela down?

Camela lowered her head and wept softly. The sound tore at Katie's heart. She shoved her hands deep into her pockets and kicked at the grass. Her dad was always fond of saying, *"Practice what you preach."* Camela had risked so much to gain back her self-confidence. *Should I be allowed to do anything less?* Katie asked herself.

Katie reached her fingers through the fence, wrapping them around Camela's. "I'll do it," she said, determined. Just the sight of all the faces brightening was worth the cost she might pay if she goofed this race.

"Jason's on the back side getting King ready," John said. "I'll go make the jockey change and let him know you'll be riding. I still think you're the best choice for King, Katie. Don't sell yourself short."

Katie gave him a nervous smile and went back to the jockeys' room to change into her silks. She was riding in the Kentucky Derby after all.

It felt like an eternity as Katie stared out at the gray clouds and steady drizzle while she waited for the paddock call. *Isn't it supposed to be sunny for the Derby?* she thought.

She checked the program for the field. There were no other women in the race. Only three women jockeys had ever ridden in the Kentucky Derby, and none of them had placed higher than eleventh. Could she be the first woman jockey to win the Kentucky Derby?

Several reporters had come to the jockeys' quarters to ask Katie for an interview now that she was riding King, but they had been turned away. No outsider was allowed into the jockeys' room until after the races.

The call came for the riders to enter the paddock. Katie jumped in her chair, a thousand butterflies taking flight in her stomach. It was time to mount up and ride in the post parade.

Katie told herself to relax as she made her way to the paddock. She spotted her mother, Jan, and Camela on the fence and forced a smile, but she was sure it looked sickly.

"Take it easy, Katie," Jason said as she entered the saddling stall. "You'll do great. Just remember how much King trusts you. You two have come a long way together. This is your moment."

John legged her up on King and gave the instructions as he walked her to the pony-horse. "The track's an awful mess, Katie girl, but the footing underneath all that slop is still pretty good. This is the biggest field of horses this colt has ever run in. We can't afford to get caught up in traffic today."

Katie nodded and patted King's neck. "The other jockeys say the track's the best about five feet off the rail," she said.

"Then that's where we need to be," John agreed. "We're going to try something different today. I want this colt to run a little closer to the front of the pack. That means you won't have as much kick at the end, but you'll also be less likely to get boxed in. Start moving him at the half-mile pole, and ask him for everything he's got at the head of the stretch."

Katie knotted her reins and positioned her feet in the irons. The saddle creaked and gave an odd pop when she stood in the stirrups to test her balance. "I'll do my best, John."

The old trainer smiled. "Don't listen to those other people who say you don't have a chance. You can do this, Katie. Nobody but a small handful of us ever believed you two would make it this far. No matter where you run in this race, you're a winner. I'll see you at the finish line."

Katie stared out over the crowd as the horses paraded down the track. The grandstands and infield were a solid mass of multicolored umbrellas. Those unfortunate enough to have forgotten their rain gear used their programs to ward off the steady drops.

They finished the parade and cantered back to the starting gate. Since the race was a mile and a quarter in distance, the horses would break from the gate at the top of the stretch, pass the finish line at the start of the race, and then pass it once again on the final run to the wire.

As they circled behind the gate, Katie could hear the excited hum of the crowd. They sounded like a million bumblebees in flight. The gateman called King's number. Katie's heart skipped a beat, then pounded loudly in her ears, but she got herself under control and urged King toward the starting gate.

"This is it, boy," Katie said as she reached down to pat King's neck. "This is what we've trained for. Let's show them an Oregon horse isn't afraid of a little rain."

There were thirteen more horses to be loaded in, so Katie took the time to recheck her equipment. The cold rain trickled down the back of her neck and chilled her fingers. She took turns holding the reins with one hand while warming the other under her arm. She wished she had thought to wear gloves like some of the other jockeys.

"Three more back," a gateman shouted.

Katie pulled down her goggles. She had five sets of them stacked one on top of the other. As sloppy as the track was today, she'd probably need all five. She looked around her, and a tingle of excitement ran down her spine. She was riding in the Kentucky Derby!

"All in. This is the moment you've been waiting for, ladies and gentlemen. Get ready to roll!" the starter yelled.

Katie jiggled King's reins, getting his attention focused down the track. A second later the bell rang, sending all sixteen horses out to fight for position in the 126th running of the Kentucky Derby.

Katie broke with the pack. She smooched to King and tapped him with her whip, moving him into position several feet off the rail. Just as John had predicted, the outside speed horses passed them up and went right to the front. Katie gasped as the cold mud splattered her face and chest. Her mouth quickly filled with sand. She snapped it shut and breathed through her nose.

They passed the grandstand on the way to the first turn. The roar of the crowd mingled with the shouts of jockeys and the thundering of hooves, making a cacophonous sound in her ears. As they entered the first turn, Katie sat low over King's withers, holding him to a constant pace that kept him in the top third of the field.

She pulled down her first set of goggles, wondering how King was able to see through all the flying mud. Her second pair was quickly filling up. At this rate she would use all five of them before they reached the homestretch. Without the goggles to keep the mud from her eyes, she'd have a hard time seeing where they were going.

They passed the three-quarters marker on the back side of the track. She drew down another set of goggles. She knew she had to find a place to run away from all the flying mud.

Katie started to pull King to the outside, but another horse moved up to block her path. She was boxed in with nowhere to go but the deep inside rail. If she moved King to the inside, it would take twice the effort to keep up with the horses running on the more solid part of the track. She pulled down her fourth set of goggles and decided to stay where she was for the moment.

They passed the half-mile pole. It was time to make her move, but Katie had no place to run. The front horses were beginning to fade, and she could see small holes opening up here and there. If she could just squeeze King into one of them, the other horses might make room. But if they didn't make room, the stewards could charge her with interference and disqualify King from the race—even if he won.

Katie pulled down her fifth set of goggles and watched for a hole to open. She readied her whip and stared through the flying mud. A patch of daylight opened, and she flagged King with the whip, driving him into the momentarily opened spot. He responded with a surge of speed, making his way between two other mounts without touching either of them. He nosed ahead of them, and suddenly they were in the clear, with only four other horses to catch.

They rounded the turn and headed into the home-stretch. The roar of the crowd was deafening. She was now directly behind the two lead horses. The mud continued to blind her. Katie reached up to clear her last set of goggles with her hand but only managed to smear the mud and make it worse.

"And it's Classical Bob in the lead by a head with World Ruler running second. Willow King is making a drive on the inside," the announcer blared over the speaker.

Katie pulled off her last set of goggles. "Come on, King, we can do this!" she screamed over the noise of the crowd. She saw the big horse's ears flick at the sound of her voice, and King pushed steadily on, valiantly trying to catch the leaders. The flying slop beat against Katie's face, burning into her eyes and rendering her almost blind.

Katie could make out the shapes of the horses in front of her and knew that King was catching up to them. She scrubbed her hands up and down King's neck and spoke to him, asking for more speed. King responded and drew abreast of the two leaders. Katie wiped at her eyes, looking for a pole that would tell her how far they had to go.

The one-eighth-mile pole flew past just as Katie heard the sound of ripping leather and was thrown forward onto King's neck. She had broken an iron!

King bobbled beside the two other horses, and for a moment Katie thought she would be dumped beneath the hooves of the charging animals. But King suddenly tossed his head into the air, and Katie flopped back into the saddle and kicked her other foot from the remaining iron.

She heard the collective gasp from the crowd as she regained her balance and sat bareback-style on her mount. There was no time for thinking. They had already lost two lengths, and another horse had moved up to challenge them for third place. As long as the jockey was still on the horse's back, the race was legal.

Katie leaned low and clamped her legs against King's sides. If she fell off at this pace, with the rest of the field running behind her, she wouldn't survive. Her whip had been lost in the mishap, so Katie had to rely on her voice and hands to inspire King to run.

The crowd went wild when she picked up her reins and pumped them along King's neck, asking him for everything he had. "Come on, boy. This is it. Get up!"

King pinned his ears, responding to her voice as his legs worked like pistons, splashing through the mud. With less than a sixteenth of a mile to go, they were drawing close to the tails of the leading horses. The sound of King's heavy breaths blew back to her ears. She knew that her beloved horse was giving her all he had.

For a moment, they hung in position, neither gaining nor losing ground. Then the outside horse dropped back, failing to retain his speed. It was just King and the leader. Katie pushed King to the limit, shouting words of encouragement she hoped he could hear over the roar of the crowd.

With great effort, King lengthened his stride and pushed ahead. He gained ground, his powerful stride eating up the muddy track below him. They were running almost neck and neck with the other horse. But when the camera flashed at the finish line, Katie knew the other rider had won.

Two strides later, King passed the winning colt, leaving no doubt in anyone's mind that he was every bit as good as the big-name horses in the race. Despite the danger of her situation, Katie laughed and raised her right hand in a victory pose. Willow King, the unknown horse from Oregon, had just made an incredible Derby run!

When the outrider pulled alongside to help pull King up, Katie hung on for dear life. The pickup horse threw his shoulder into King and almost unseated her.

"I've never seen anything like that," laughed the outrider. "This one will go down in history. Not only are you the first female jockey to place this high in the Derby, you're definitely the first jockey to do it without irons!"

Katie rode up to the unsaddling area, waving to the stewards to show that she didn't claim any fouls.

Jason ran up to grab King's reins. "Wow, that was a great race, Kat," he said, amazed. "You and King just ran second!"

"Just a minute there," John warned as he pulled the broken stirrup from the saddle. "The stewards haven't posted the official sign yet. That was a mighty strange finish. They're probably looking at the tape to make sure there wasn't any interference with the other horses."

Katie steadied the blowing horse and looked over her shoulder to see King's number flash second on the tote board. The crowd let out a whoop loud enough to make King shy. She laughed and hugged his muddy neck. "We gave them a run for their money, didn't we, boy?"

Cameras flashed and videotape rolled as the media crowded outside the fence, hoping to get a good shot of the amazing duo. They were getting almost as much attention as the winners.

Katie's mother and Jan, along with Camela and the Ellis family, waded through the throng, pushing their way to the track fence to shout their congratulations.

Katie didn't know whether to laugh or cry when the winning jockey plucked a single rose from the blanket of roses placed over the winning horse's withers and tossed it to her, shouting that she and King had run a great race.

Katie jumped down from King's back and wiped her eyes. She brushed some of the mud off her face, then smiled so broadly that it hurt. The flash of a camera momentarily blinded her, but she could still see the smiles of her friends and family.

Jason held King's reins, giving the big bay colt a solid pat as he praised him. Then he handed the reins over to John and picked Katie up, twirling her around with a shout before he set her back in the mud and took the reins back from John.

The old trainer handed Katie a handkerchief. "Well, Katie girl, you and King did it! Now where do we go from here?"

Katie took the rose the jockey had given her and

brought it to her nose. Everyone waited for her answer. She leaned down and placed the rose in Camela's hair. "I'm not sure," Katie said with a smile. "But next time, I think I'll try it with stirrups!"

Katie hummed a tune as she stared out over the pine-dotted Oregon landscape, remembering all the details from the Kentucky Derby the week before. She finished brushing King's glossy coat and tossed the brushes into the box just as she heard footsteps coming up the aisle. Poking her head out of the stall, she saw Jason escort Camela down the shed row.

"John got a letter from Mark in the hospital," said Jason. "His leg is healing well, and he should be up and walking in a few days. He'll be riding again next month."

"That's good news," said Katie. "He looked pretty beat up after the accident."

"He says congratulations, by the way," said Jason.

Katie and Jason looked at each other for a few moments. Nothing needed to be said between them. They both just knew that they were a great team and would always be one. Jason walked over to King and patted his neck, while Katie made her way to Camela. "It's so good to see you, Cam," Katie said as she sat beside her friend on their usual bale of straw. "You haven't been around much since we got back from Kentucky. I've missed you."

Camela smiled in delight. "I've missed you too, but you're the reason I haven't been around much."

"Did I rush you too fast on the horses?" Katie frowned in concern. "I didn't mean to scare you off."

"No, no, it had nothing to do with the horses." Camela

219

laughed. "I'm really proud of you for riding in the Kentucky Derby, even though I know how scared you were. You really inspired me. I was thinking about what you said about my education and how important it is." Camela pulled a piece of straw from the bale and fumbled with it. "I've really been cutting corners on my education," she said. "I'm so far behind that I've got a whole lot of work to do to catch up. I haven't been around much because I've been working double-time with my tutor."

"That's great, Cam. I'm proud of you."

"It's all because of you, Katie," Camela said, smiling.

Katie reached out to hug the young girl, feeling the warm glow of pride fill her. "Naw, it was in you all the time, Cam. I just helped drag it out."

Camela laughed, then grew serious. "I'm going home tomorrow."

Katie felt as if someone had punched her. She exhaled a measured breath. "So soon?"

Camela nodded. "But school's almost over, and my aunt and uncle have invited me back to stay the summer. Even Cindy asked me to come back." Camela snickered, then quickly sobered. "Will it be okay if I come back to help you and King, Katie?"

Katie wiped a tear from her eye. "Of course it will. You've been like a sister."

"A bratty one, no doubt," Camela said, giggling. "Who knows, you might even talk me into riding," she added.

"Challenge accepted!" Katie exclaimed.

Camela picked up her cane and stood. "I've got to get going. There's lots of packing to be done."

"Let me walk you back to the house," offered Jason. But

to their surprise, Camela declined.

"Don't be so shocked," Camela admonished. "A couple of times late at night, when nobody else was around, I had Cindy bring me down here so I could find my way back on my own." She reached out for Katie's hand. "Aside from the great friendship we share, Katie, that's one thing I'll always be grateful to you for."

"What's that?" Katie was confused.

"You've given me back my independence," Camela said as she gave Katie a big hug.

Katie smiled. "You gave me something important too," she said to her friend, holding her tight. "You reminded me that I need to trust and believe in myself. Thanks for talking me into riding King in the Derby."

Katie released her hold on Camela. Jason smiled at her and held Katie's hand as they watched their friend make her own way down the shed row, tapping her cane and stopping here and there to feel for a landmark that would let her know exactly where she was.

King popped his head over the stall door and pushed his muzzle against Katie's shoulder. Katie stepped to his stall and threw her arms around the big colt's neck. "If there's one thing I've learned from all of this," she said with a smile, "it's that the winner isn't always the one who crosses the finish line first."

King agreed by giving Katie a soft whinny that tickled her ear.